A COUNTRY MUSIC CHRISTMAS
by
Maggie Carpenter

Cover Image
Dark Secrets Press
Published by: Dark Secrets Press
http://www.MaggieCarpenter.com
https://www.facebook.com/MaggieCarpenterWriter
https://twitter.com/magcarpenter2

CHAPTER ONE

Summer froze, then sharply pulling her phone from her ear she searched for an excuse.

"Summer? Summer are you there?"

Her thumb automatically slipped over the OFF icon, and dropping the phone on the table, she slowly turned around. Liam was moving towards her wearing a dark frown, his milk chocolate eyes narrowing, and his full lips grimly pressed together. She was screwed. Absolutely, one-thousand-percent screwed.

"I-uh—"

"Don't even try," he growled, "I've heard enough. When you came knockin' on my door lookin' for a job you were here for one reason and one reason only! A record deal. You lied to me."

Summer had never felt her heart pump so fast, nor her face burn so hot.

"And what about all those cozy talks we've been havin'," he demanded, drawing closer, "and the flirtin' in your painted-on jeans? Damn, all this time you've been playin' me. Totally playin' me."

She could hear the hurt in his voice. It was killing her. She may have arrived on his doorstep wanting to be the next Taylor Swift, and she still did, but in the three months she'd been there she'd fallen for him, and hard.

He stopped directly in front of her.

His cologne tickled her nostrils.

She loved the smell.

A few weeks earlier she'd sneaked home one of his T-shirts, and each night she'd crawl into bed, closed her eyes, and inhaled the spicy, musky fragrance as she danced her fingers against her sex.

Suddenly it happened.

The glorious unthinkable.

Without warning his fingers clutched her hair, he tugged back her head, and his lips were devouring hers. She couldn't breathe, her stomach was alive with a thousand butterflies, and her heart somersaulted against her chest. But just as abruptly he broke away, and to her horror, with a life of its own, her hand unexpectedly flew from her side and slapped him.

"Oh, my gosh, Liam, I'm so sorry. I don't know why I did that."

But his eyes blazed down at her. She needed to escape, to run, to hide.

"You think offense is gonna be your defense? That's not gonna work on me, Summer Brown."

With an alacrity that startled her, he bent her over and landed his hand on her backside with a flurry of hard swats. The short sharp spanking lasted only seconds, but when he set her on her feet her backside was hot and stinging.

"H-how d-dare you?" she railed, but her voice had sounded thin, and when she'd stammered her protest her eyes had been glued to the floor.

"Look at me," he said sternly. "Right now! Look at me!"

"No!"

"Summer!"

"After what you just did I don't want to look at you. Why would I?"

"Because I'm tellin' you to, and from where I'm standin' it seems like the smart thing to do."

Swallowing hard, she slowly raised her head.

"Did you really think if you were singin' while you were workin' I'd walk up and say, hey, girl, that's a real pretty voice you got? Did you think I'd magically sign you to a million dollar record contract? Is that what you were thinkin' when you lied your way into a job here?"

"Something like that," she murmured, then feeling an unexpected spark of defiance, she tilted up her chin and glared at him. "How else could I get you to hear me? I can't afford to cut a demo, but dammit I can sing. I can sing anyone under the table."

Her voice had risen in pitch and volume, but she knew she'd been wrong to deceive him. At any time over the last three months she could have admitted why she'd knocked on his door in the first place, and politely asked if she could audition.

"Honey, that's a fairytale," he said solemnly. "I don't mean to be unkind, but there are thousands of pretty girls with pretty voices, and a whole bunch of them have come into my life believin' if they sang a few bars I'd fall over myself to get their name on the dotted line. It doesn't work that way."

"But..."

"But, nothin'!"

An awkward silence fell between them, and needing to shift her gaze from his scolding glare she glanced across at the window. In spite of the circumstances she broke into a smile. Snow!

"I guess the storm they talked about is comin' in," he remarked, following her gaze. "This place is gonna have a white Christmas. I think you'd better leave."

"You're not firing me, are you?"

* * *

Liam thrust his hands in his pockets. That's not what he'd meant, though the thought had crossed his mind. The forecasters had warned of heavy weather and he wanted to make sure she was home before the roads became dangerous.

"I'm sorry, honestly, I really like working here," she said earnestly, "and, uh, I really like you."

He turned and looked back at her. There had been a hot chemistry between them from the moment they'd laid eyes on each other, but moments before he'd heard her on the phone saying she'd been singing up a storm all morning hoping he'd notice her voice. A surge of anger had rippled through him. She'd lied, but she'd looked so damn gorgeous, her face flushed and her honey-blond hair falling around her shoulders, the impulsive kiss had taken hold before he'd been able to stop himself. He almost couldn't blame her for slapping him. He'd blindsided her.

"Please, Liam, please tell me I'm not fired. I'm truly sorry."

"I need to think about this, and you'd better go before—what the hell is that?"

A series of beeps filled the room, and he realized his many electronic gadgets were shutting down.

"Oh my gosh. The power's off already?" Summer exclaimed. "How could that be?"

"It doesn't matter. I have a generator. It should kick in pretty quick."

"Thank goodness. We have one too. With dad being away so much he insisted on it."

"You'd best get home," he declared as everything clicked back on.

"But, uh, am I fired?"

"I said I need to think about it. Lyin' for three months? That doesn't sit well with me."

"You just kissed me and whacked my ass! Maybe that doesn't sit well with me either!"

"Is that right?" he demanded, fresh anger rising up. "Are you sayin' you didn't want me to kiss you? Are you tellin' me you didn't like it? Why the sudden silence? You've had a lot to say for yourself up 'til now."

"Let's just say it was unexpected."

"That's about as evasive as a slick-tongued salesman, but at least it wasn't a lie. Now go and have a happy Christmas with your family. I'll think about all this over the holiday."

"How can I have a happy Christmas with this hanging over my head? That's not fair."

Liam paused. She was right.

"Call me in the mornin'. I'll be leavin' for Nashville around ten."

"I am sorry, Liam."

"I know," he sighed, hearing the regret in her voice. "I'll walk you outside."

They were in his den, a masculine man-cave with wood paneled walls, coffered ceilings, recessed lights, an antique desk, and a dark brown leather chesterfield sofa that sat in front of a fireplace.

"Liam, can I say something?"

"Sure. Say whatever you want."

"This is my favorite room. It looks like you, and the platinum and gold records mounted on the walls, and the line of Grammys on the fireplace mantle...they're inspiring. It must be amazing to sell millions of records and accept a Grammy. I dream about it all the time."

"Takes a lotta hard work to get there, so yeah, it's a great feelin," he said as they started down the hall.

"My dad says if you love something it's not work."

"What does your dad do?"

"He's a marine," she replied as they lifted their coats off the rack by the door. "Didn't I tell you? He's home for the holidays."

"Nope," he said, opening the door. "You should be proud. Tell him Merry Christmas from me, and thank him for his service."

"I will. Wow, it's falling fast!"

"I should take you home in my Rover."

"I'll be fine. I'm used to this, besides, I have a Subaru and it's not far."

"Be careful, drive slow, and call me the minute you get home."

Firmly gripping her elbow he walked her down the front steps to her car and opened the door.

"Remember, call me when you get home!"

"I promise," she said, climbing in behind the wheel.

Shutting her door, he hurried back to the protection of his porch, staying there to make sure the tall, iron gates opened, then moved quickly back inside. Pulling off his jacket he strode to his kitchen, poured himself some hot coffee, and sat down on the padded bench seat in the breakfast nook. The bay window overlooked his backyard, and the expansive lawn was quickly turning white. Reaching for the phone he called the local airport.

"Apple Valley Air."

"Hey, Wally, it's Liam Taylor. Am I gonna be able to take off tomorrow?"

"Doubtful. The storm developed bigger and quicker than anyone forecast."

"What if I raced out there now?"

"Hmm, maybe. Hold on."

Liam began drumming his fingers on the tabletop. He wasn't far from the airfield, and his jet was a Gulfstream G550.

"We're good for about an hour then we'll be closing down."

Thanks, Wally. I'm goin' for it."

"I'll call Frank and let him know, then see if I can scout out a co-pilot," Wally offered. "I'm sure I'll be able to rustle up someone."

Frank was Liam's pilot, an ex-naval officer who had once been a Top Gun. He wasn't just an outstanding flyer, he had become one of Liam's closest friends.

"Thanks, Wally. I'll throw a few things together and head out there. I'll see you shortly."

Trotting up the stairs to his bedroom, he placed his half-packed suitcase on the bed and hurriedly threw in the last few bits and pieces. There were gifts that still needed wrapping, something he'd planned to do that night, but he could have fun recruiting his niece and nephew to help.

Quickly changing, he carried his bags into the garage and placed them in the back of his Range Rover, then heading back inside he returned to his den to make sure he hadn't forgotten anything, but as he stood behind his desk, the kiss flashed through his head. It had sparked his cock to life, and he'd loved smacking her ass. Summer was a sassy spitfire. He'd fantasized about throwing her over his knee and baring her backside more than once.

Shaking off the salacious thoughts, he glanced at his watch. It had been twenty-minutes since he'd watched her car disappear through the gates. She'd often told him her house was just through town. He should have heard from her.

"Dammit," he muttered, pulling his phone from his pocket. "I'd better just make sure you made it back safely before I take off."

The sound of Blake Shelton's voice unexpectedly filled the air.

Summer's ringtone.

Glancing across the room, he saw her phone sitting on a side table.

CHAPTER TWO

Cursing himself for not having Summer's home number, and not wanting to waste precious time trying to track it down, Liam decided to call directory assistance on the way to the airfield.

"I should take her phone with me and ask Wally to get it to her," he muttered, staring at the phone in its sparkly pink cover. "Yeah. I'll be gone at least two weeks and she'll need it."

Dropping it into his briefcase, he hurried into the foyer, set the house alarm, and strode quickly through the kitchen and into the garage. Hitting the remote control button on the wall as he entered, he paused for a moment to glance out at the weather. He grimaced. The snow was no longer floating down, but being driven by gusting winds.

Climbing behind the wheel of his powerful 4WD Rover, he dropped his briefcase on the passenger seat, and as he cautiously backed out, he wondered if the trip to the airfield would be a waste of time.

Putting his SUV into four-wheel drive, he drove carefully down his driveway, through the gates and onto the road. His home was set on a knoll, and rolling carefully down the hill he could see red brake lights ahead, but as he drew closer, he discovered the car was nose-down in a ditch. Stopping and lowering his window, he peered through the swirling snow.

To his horror, it was Summer's subaru.

Urgently touching the phone pad on his console he dialed 911, but the call didn't connect. Glancing at the screen he realized there was no service. Cursing under his breath, he drove forward to the narrow shoulder and hurriedly climbed out. As he started back towards her car, he noticed the incline beside him was gently sloped, but the car was stuck down a sharp drop. Worried he wouldn't be able to reach Summer from the road, he trudged carefully into the ravine. Tramping forward, he tried to hasten his step, but the side of the bank was becoming perilously steep, and with the wind and snow billowing around him it was difficult to keep his balance.

Trying to control his mounting panic, he pushed ahead, slipping and sliding on the icy bank. He was getting closer, but as he scrambled the last few yards to the driver's door, his foot caught on a snow-covered rock. Pitching forward, he fell violently against the side of the car banging his elbow. Doing his best to ignore a shard of painful tingles through his forearm, he regained his balance, grabbed the roof rack with one hand, and the door handle with the other. Though the door creaked in protest, with a couple of strong tugs it finally opened. His heart thundering, he lowered his head and looked inside; Summer's tear stained face and wide eyes stared back at him.

"Liam, th-thank G-God."

"Are you hurt?"

"N-no, I don't think so. Just f-freaked out and f-freezing. Sh-shaky, you know? I'm all sh-shaky. I c-couldn't get the d-door open and my ph-phone, it's not in my p-pocket. Liam...I thought I was going to d-die here."

"I'm going to get you out, but the bank is steep, and slippery, real slippery. You've gotta be careful."

Peering past him, she saw the perilous path.

"Sh-shit. How will I b-be able to g-get th-through there? It's s-straight down."

"Only for a short distance then it levels out."

"My b-bag," she muttered, turning her head to look at the passenger seat.

"Does it have a shoulder strap?"

"Uh-huh. Liam, I'm s-scared, and m-my legs f-feel all wobbly. I'll n-never m-make it."

"Let me see if I can get to the other side of the car. Maybe it's not as bad. Wait there."

"W-wait? Where w-would I g-go?"

Her quick retort was the last thing he'd expected, but it was reassuring. Struggling to the front of the car, he clambered on top of the sawed off tree trunk she'd hit. It was tall and wide, and he could view the opposite side of the ditch. The slope was kinder. Greatly relieved, he made his way to the passenger door. To his surprise it opened without a fight.

"It's better on this side," he said, but as he extended his hand to help her, a powerful blast of wind gusted around him. The storm was strengthening. Glancing up at the overhead trees, he could easily imagine the branches breaking away. "Summer, we need to get outta here."

"I have n-no d-desire to stay, b-believe me," she stammered, climbing over the console.

The car suddenly creaked .

"Wh-what was th-that?" she exclaimed, panic written across her face."It's g-going to f-fall down the b-bank!"

"It's okay, it's stuck, you're fine, keep comin'."

"Shit, shit, shit."

"You can swear all you want, just keep comin'."

"F-fuck, this is horrible."

"That's it, you're almost here," he said confidently, helping her out of the crunched car.

Picking up her bag and throwing it over his shoulder, he placed an arm around her waist and they started off, but after climbing up the bank to the road, he could see she was on her last legs. Swooping her up, he carried her through the wild weather to his car. Setting her on her feet to open the passenger door, he tossed his briefcase on the floor, and deposited her bag on top of it.

"In you go."

"I'm s-so c-cold," she quaked as she struggled into the SUV. "I c-can't f-feel m-my hands or f-feet."

"I have a blanket in the back and the car has heated seats. Just hold on."

Slamming the door shut, he hurried to open his tail gate, and grabbing the thick thermal rug, he moved swiftly to the driver's side and climbed inside.

"I c-can't b-believe how b-bad this storm is," she muttered as he handed her the blanket. "Ooh, thank you. I'm t-totally f-frozen."

"The heater will soon warm you up, and you need to take slow, deep breaths."

Starting up the powerful engine, he hit the button to heat the seats, then sat for moment to catch his breath.

"L-Liam, I was s-so s-scared," she stammered, fresh tears spilling down her face.

"Of course you were, but you're safe now. We're goin' back to my place. I don't think I should be drivin' anywhere in this mess."

Rolling forward, he turned his car around. Worried tree limbs might be littering the roa, he took his time, and his concern was justified. As they neared the tall gates fronting his driveway he had to maneuver around several branches. The short drive had felt like forever, and finally pulling to a stop inside his garage, as the door closed behind him, he leaned back in his seat and let out a long breath.

"I can't believe you found me," Summer said softly. The powerful heater and hot seats had worked their magic. Her teeth had stopped chattering and her voice, though thin, sounded almost normal. "You saved my life."

"I'm sure your parents would have sent someone to look for you."

"But not until tonight. I'm supposed to be here all day working, remember?" she sniffled, fresh tears dribbling down her face. "You did, Liam, you saved my life."

"Never mind about that now," he murmured, pulling off his gloves and reaching across the console to wipe away her tears. "I'm just glad you're safe. We'll go inside and you can take a hot bath."

"I don't have any clothes."

"I'll take you to the second bedroom upstairs. You'll find whatever you need in there. Take as long as you like. It's not like we can go anywhere."

As he climbed out and walked around the Rover to open her door, the words rang in his head.

It's not like we can go anywhere.

It was true, and there was no way of knowing how long they'd be stranded. Opening her door and helping her out, all sorts of possibilities sprang to mind. She glanced up at him.

"Liam?"

"Yes, Summer?"

"I don't know how I'll ever be able to thank you."

"You can thank me by taking a hot bath right away. You're much too pale."

As she walked ahead of him towards the door, a grin crossed his face. Sometimes fate was kind, and he suspected the near disaster could well be a blessing in disguise.

essing in disguise.

CHAPTER THREE

Closing her eyes, Summer sank into the warm foamy water. Even though she was safe and out of the wretched cold, she could still feel the threat of tears. The guest room was the one Liam's sister used when she visited, and Liam had told her to help herself to whatever she needed.

There were clean clothes in the chest of drawers and hanging in the closet, and plenty of creams and cosmetics in the bathroom cabinets. He'd also told her to add hot water slowly, as her body thawed.

Thawed!

It had been an appropriate word. She'd felt as if she was a block of ice when she'd climbed into the tub.

She dunked her head back, then rising up, she wiped her face and turned on the hot faucet. Liam was her hero, and she hated herself for deceiving him. Would she ever be able to win back his trust? She doubted it. He'd been absolutely furious, and on top of that she'd slapped him! Groaning as the moment replayed itself in her mind's eye, she wondered why she'd done such a thing. She had dreamed about him planting his lips on hers more times than she could count, and the real thing had been amazing.

Then there was the spanking!

She'd been stunned when he'd bent her over and smacked her, but in retrospect she knew she'd deserved every swat.

"Liam," she mumbled, "if only you knew how much I care about you. I'm such an idiot, such a total fucking idiot."

She'd been crazy about Liam Taylor even before they'd met. He was as famous as his celebrity clients, and had been labeled country music's Simon Cowell. The title was fitting. Not only did Liam possess an uncanny ability to spot talented artists and develop them, he had Simon Cowell's unnerving penchant for stating the obvious, both the good and the bad. She'd spent hours watching his television specials and reading interviews, and though she'd known he'd spent time in her small town growing up, she'd never imagined he'd return. When she'd heard he'd purchased a vacation home in the hills just beyond Main Street, she'd been ecstatic.

Then determination set in.

He had to hear her sing.

She'd had the vision.

She was going to be a star.

Her visions were rare, but frighteningly accurate. They would appear during sleep, but she knew how to recognize her premonitions, and not confuse them with dreams. The unique gift had been inherited from her father. She loved him deeply, and was immensely proud of him, but she hated his deployments. He'd be gone for long months, but she came to understand his patriotism, and his need to fight for his country. When he was home, they'd sit on the balcony he'd built for her off her bedroom window and talk for hours. It was also where she'd sought his advice about singing for Liam.

"How do I meet him, dad?" she'd asked earnestly. "He has to hear me sing. He just has to."

"You know where he lives. Why don't you knock on his door? What's the worst than can happen?"

"Knock on his door!" she'd exclaimed, completely aghast at the suggestion. "But that's impossible. First of all, there is no door, just a huge gate, and second of all, even if I was lucky enough to see him, what would I say?"

"Nice to meet you, Mr. Taylor. My name is Summer Brown. Everyone says I have a voice as strong as Adele's and as sweet as Taylor Swift's. Please may I sing for you? That's how you do it. Straightforward and honest."

"I couldn't...could I?"

"Hey, kitten, the man's always lookin' for talent, and you've got it in spades. He sure isn't gonna hear you if you stay stuck in your bedroom wishin' and hopin'."

"You're right about that."

"Sometimes in life you gotta take a deep breath and go for it."

As she recalled the conversation, she wanted to kick herself. Why hadn't she done exactly as her father had suggested?

But she knew why.

The brave, determined, nothing's-going-to-stop-me Summer Brown had choked.

When the amazing, talented, handsome Liam Taylor had been the one to answer the gate intercom, she'd been so shocked she'd heard herself say something she'd not even considered until that very moment.

"Hi, my name is Summer Brown, and I wondered, since you just moved in, if you needed any help, like, a personal assistant kind of help."

She'd stammered her way through the lie, and though there'd been no verbal response, the gates had opened. Driving nervously up the sweeping driveway, she'd stopped beneath the portico, and when she'd stepped from her car, he'd been standing at the open door. Seeing him in the flesh with his dazzling smile and looking ridiculously gorgeous, she'd totally and completely lost her nerve.

The water was growing tepid, but as a wave of emotion took hold, she barely noticed. She'd smashed up her car, but far worse, she was crazy about a man completely out of her league, and her dreams of singing for him felt further away than ever.

"I suppose I should be counting my blessings," she mumbled. "If he hadn't come along I'd still be in that car and frozen to death. I need to apologize profusely, thank him one more time for saving me, and when the storm's over, I'll promise never to bother him again."

* * *

At the end of the hall behind double-doors that led into the master bedroom, Liam had stepped from a long hot shower and was toweling off. He was the king of long hot showers. It was where he did his best thinking. The water seemed to wash away the fog and crystalize his ideas. Even at his Nashville headquarters, he had a shower next to his office. If his secretary walked in and his desk chair was empty, she knew he'd be in the bathroom standing under a stream of steaming water.

The shower had once again done its job. He knew exactly what he needed to do and exactly how to do it, and he also guessed why Summer had lied to him when she'd first arrived at his door. She'd been courageous enough to pull up to his gate, but once standing in front of him she'd lost her nerve.

Donning a comfortable pair of black slacks and a dark green sweater, he slipped his feet into moccasin slippers, then headed quickly down the stairs and into his den. Picking up his landline phone, he wasn't surprised to find no dial tone. Moving behind his desk he powered up his computer, and fully expecting to find no internet, he was pleasantly surprised to discover it working. Sitting down, he immediately sent an email to Frank and Wally letting them know he was safe and at home, and he had neither cell service or a landline.

But he was cloaked in disappointment.

He wouldn't be with his family for Christmas.

Walking into the large living room he turned on the fire, then ambled into the kitchen and placed his mug under the built-in coffee maker. Choosing Dark French Roast, he remembered Summer liked the mild Colombian, and made a mug for her. Dropping a splash of whiskey in both, he topped them with fresh whipped cream. That was another of his indulgences. Heavy whipping cream. The real stuff. His favorite was from King Island in the South Pacific.

"I feel almost human again."

Summer's voice caught his attention. Turning around, he saw her walking slowly towards him dressed in a pale pink velvet sweat suit, and thick, white woolly socks. Her hair, still wet from her bath, fell carelessly around her shoulders, and there was not a stitch of makeup on her face. She looked innocent and vulnerable, and absolutely beautiful.

"You look a whole lot more than almost human," he murmured with a smile. "How do you feel?"

"Compared to how I felt a little while ago, positively wonderful. My body is aching a bit, but otherwise I'm fine."

"I just made some coffee with a drop of whisky. That should take the last of the chill from your bones."

"That sounds perfect, thank you," she said gratefully, picking up the mug and taking a sip. "Did you say a drop?"

"Okay, maybe a hair more than a drop."

"Are the phones working? I need to call home and let mom and dad know what happened."

"Sadly no, but the internet's still up. You can shoot them an email."

"Really? That's a surprise. Thank you, I will, but I'll drink this first."

"Let's sit by the fire in the livin' room. There's something I need to talk with you about."

"Sure," she replied, but her heart began to sink. Was this going to be the, I'm sorry, Summer, I'll make sure you get home safe, but your days here are over speech?

Walking through the elegant dining room and down the hall, they moved under the arch that led into the living room. It offered a cozy conversation pit around a large fireplace, and settling into the comfortable couch, she took a sip of dutch courage before placing her mug on the coffee table.

She was ready.

If he fired her, which she expected, she'd do her best not to cry, and make sure he knew she was deeply ashamed and very sorry.

"Have you made up your mind," she asked tentatively, "about me working here I mean?"

"I have, and, yeah, I'm gonna fire you."

CHAPTER FOUR

Though she'd been expecting it, the impact of his words was like a fist landing in her gut, and in spite of promising herself she wouldn't cry, a burning brick of lava sprung to life at the back of her throat.

"You have no idea how much I regret what I did," she managed, "and not just because I'm losing a job I love. I'm not a deceitful person, and now you think I am. That's the worst thing of all. I could give you a bunch of excuses, but like my dad says, excuses don't change anything."

"Your dad sounds like a smart guy, but I'm not firin' you 'cos you lied to me. Everyone's entitled to get cold feet. That's what happened, right?"

"Oh, my gosh. That's exactly what happened. So you understand?"

"I get it for the first couple of weeks, but Summer, three months? Anyway, that's not why I'm lettin' you go."

"Did I do something else wrong? Is it because I slapped you? I'm sorry about that too, really sorry."

"If you just stop talkin' for a minute, I'll tell you."

"Sorry. Good grief I'm saying that a lot, but I am, about everything."

"That's a start."

"A start?"

"I'm gonna make you a proposition."

"What kind of proposition?"

"First we gotta get real. Let's talk about that slap. You wanted me to kiss you and I did. Maybe it took both of us by surprise, but you couldn't deal with it, and you took your frustration and guilt out on me."

"Maybe," she said softly, dropping her eyes.

"Maybe? Coy doesn't wear well on you, sugar."

"Okay, yes, I did want you to kiss me...very much."

"Just for the record, I don't go around kissin' women willy nilly."

"Good to know," she said facetiously, raising her eyes and shooting him a sassy look.

"You're sure gettin' cocky all of a sudden."

Summer bit her lower lip.

He was right.

She was always pushing the envelope.

She just didn't know why.

"I do that," she admitted. "I feel remorseful and guilty, but then I do or say something that just makes things worse. It's as if I have an evil twin living inside me."

He smiled. He'd seen glimpses of the challenging, difficult side of her personality, but it wasn't a turn-off, not for a minute. On the contrary, he found it intriguing.

"I'm not sure I'd call her evil. Naughty, even bratty, but not evil."

"Thank you for saying that, and I'd love to hear your proposition."

"No more smart-ass remarks?"

"No more smart-ass remarks, I promise."

"You're fired because I don't become involved with my employees, and I wanna get to know you better."

"I can't believe it! Liam, I would love that."

"I wouldn't get too happy just yet. There are conditions. Don't get it into your head this is attached to a record contract. This is strictly personal. Got it?"

"Does that mean you never want to hear me sing?"

"Never's a long time, but that's not a part of this. If I'm not enough—"

"Sorry, sorry," she said quickly. "It's not that, it's—"

"Disappointing? Hey, I get it, and if bein' around me is gonna be too tough it's best we leave things as they are. Do you need time to think about it?"

"I don't need to think about anything," she said firmly, wondering what it would be like to curl up in his arms.

"There's another condition."

"I don't care what it is. I won't change my mind."

"It's not quite that simple."

"What do you mean?"

"I'm gonna start things off layin' you over my knee and givin' you a proper spankin'."

She stared at him like a deer in headlights, and a flurry of butterflies burst to life in the pit of her stomach.

"Don't you think you deserve a spankin' for connivin' the whole time you've been here? That's not cool, sugar, and if we're gonna move forward you've gotta get rid of all the guilt you're feelin'. Don't deny it, it's written all over your bright red cheeks."

"I can't stand this," she mumbled, raising her hands and covering her face.

"Hey, it's good you're embarrassed, you should be. It shows you've got a conscience."

"I guess, but you've already spanked me."

"That was for the slap!"

"Shit."

"This is how I roll, Summer. You've gotta know I don't take kindly to someone tryin' to pull the wool over my eyes. I'm not gonna let it go unpunished."

"This is crazy!" she declared, dropping her hands and staring at him.

"Nope, but you wanna know what is? No-one has ever called you on your crap."

"I don't know what you mean?"

"Tell me if this sounds familiar. You do somethin' you shouldn't, and when your fella gets mad, you roll your big blue eyes at him, press up against him and beg his forgiveness. You have great make-up sex and things go back to normal, but for some reason you find it just a bit frustratin'. How am I doin'? Is that about how things usually go?"

Summer was speechless, but her mind raced.

Everything about Liam Taylor confounded her.

What he'd just said was true, but how could he possibly know?

And how could he be so warm and yet so—what?

Strict?

Was that the word?

Strong?

No, it was more than strong.

His kiss had made her knees weak and her stomach flip, and when she'd slapped him he hadn't gotten mad or walked away, or any of the other reactions she'd expected. He'd dared to spank her, and he'd done it quickly and calmly.

Now he was threatening to do it again.

No.

He wasn't threatening, he was telling her.

He'd made it crystal clear if she wanted to spend time with him, personal, special time, he'd wallop her butt as the starting point.

"Am I right?" he pressed. "Is that how things have gone in the past?"

"Uh-huh," she mumbled, "but why are you telling me all this? I mean, what is it exactly you're trying to say? I'm confused."

"Come here," he said softly, reaching across and engulfing her in a bear hug.

She was as grateful as she was surprised, and sinking against the soft cashmere of his sweater, she let out a long, heavy sigh. Being in his arms was more divine than she'd even imagined, and she never, ever, wanted to leave them.

"I didn't mean to confuse you, Summer. I'm not like most other men."

"No kidding!"

Her quip brought a smile to his face. She was different too, and he strongly suspected she was the other side of his coin.

"I could be wrong, but I've got a sneakin' suspicion we're more compatible than you might think."

"I hope so, but regardless, I really am sorry about everything. I hope you believe me."

"Sure I believe you, but like I said, if you want us to start seein' each other, I've gotta spank that cute backside of yours. It's just the way I am, but when it's over, it'll be forgotten and we can move on."

"Liam?"

"Yep?"

"I like it here, like this, with you, in front of the fire. Can I ask a favor?"

"Sure. That's one of the things I've learned in life. Most of the time if you ask, you get."

"Are you saying if I'd asked you to listen to me sing when I first arrived you would have? Wait, don't answer that. I don't want to know."

"What's the favor?"

"Will you kiss me again?"

"Hell, yeah, I'll kiss you again."

He hadn't smiled when he'd said it, and as he lowered his lips on to hers, she felt a warm delicious flood between her legs. She abruptly realized she couldn't wait to feel his hot hand smack her butt again.

"So," he said softly as he pulled back, "anything to say?"

"More than I could possibly manage."

"I'm not sure what that means."

"It means yes, I accept your conditions, but I think I'm going to need to finish that coffee."

"Why don't you take it into my den and email your folks. Let them know about the accident and that you're gonna stay here until the weather clears."

"I will, but..."

"But?"

"Liam, this is weird. It's Christmas Eve. I can hear the wind howling out there and it's only getting worse. I want to be with you, but my dad is home for the holidays and I should be there."

"That's too bad," he said with a frown. "I'm supposed to be with my family in Nashville, but that's not gonna happen either. I was on my way to the airfield when I saw your car."

"I stopped you from leaving?"

"Nope. The weather got bad. I wouldn't have been able to fly off anyway, and if I'd made it to the airfield, I would've had a helluva time gettin' back here. You wanna tell me how you ended up in that ditch?"

"It was my own stupid fault."

"Usually is. Not you, I mean generally. Most accidents happen because of human error."

"I was trying to find my phone in my bag and I hit some ice. It happened so fast. Once I was in the ditch I couldn't get my door open, and when I started to crawl over to the passenger side, the car made this awful sound. I was sure it was about to topple down the cliff. I had no idea I was crunched into a tree trunk."

"I thought I told you to drive carefully. That wasn't drivin' carefully."

"No, I guess not."

"I'm gonna have to give you a few extra swats for that."

"Oh, my gosh," she whispered, dropping her eyes. "You're really going to spank me."

"Yep, then I'm gonna hold you real tight."

"My stomach's doing cartwheels."

"You can always change your mind."

"No, no, but, uh, like you said, I should email mom and dad."

"Tell them you'll Skype them. With any luck they'll have internet too. At least you'll be able to see them when you talk to them."

"That's a super idea."

"I'm gonna fetch my luggage from the car while you're doin' that, and then, little lady, your backside has a date with my hand."

"Did you have to say that?" she mumbled, feeling a fresh flame cross her face.

"Yep. Go on, now. I'll see you back here shortly."

As Liam watched her pick up her coffee and walk away, he reached for his mug and took a long swallow. She wasn't just gorgeous, she had a smokiness in her speaking voice that suggested she really could have great chops.

Three months before, when he'd opened his front door and seen the beautiful girl step from her car, he'd immediately assumed she'd lied and was there because she was an aspiring singer. If she'd asked for an audition, he would have given her five minutes, but to his dismay she had chosen the duplicitous route. He'd invited her in because he genuinely did need help.

But he'd also felt an immediate attraction.

As the weeks had passed, that initial attraction had transformed into something much more, and when she'd stolen one of his T-shirts he'd known why. She wasn't the only one fantasizing.

"Summer, Summer," he muttered as he rose to his feet and headed to the garage, "you've got some lesson's comin'. We're in for a real interestin' time."

CHAPTER FIVE

As Liam passed through the kitchen and into the garage, he realized his luggage should stay where it was. He'd be leaving as soon as the storm broke, but he needed his briefcase. Carrying it into his den, he found Summer standing by the window watching the storm raging outside.

"It's so bad," she murmured as he walked up beside her. "I don't think I've ever seen a storm like this."

"We always say things like that about weather, but most of the time we've just forgotten."

"I suppose you're right."

"I remember some amazin' storms when I'd come here as a kid. My aunt was obsessed with weather, and whenever a storm was predicted she'd use it as an excuse to run over to Wishes Bakery and buy all kinds of cakes. She claimed she was stockin' up. It always made me laugh."

"I love that place. I wish we had some of their pies here to see us through this."

"I'm just glad the place is still in business. Apple Valley wouldn't be the same without it. When this storm is over we'll go there for coffee."

"That would be great."

"I assume you sent the email to your parents."

"I did, but I haven't heard from them yet. I hope they have internet."

"I thought you were comin' back into the living room. Why did you decide to stay in here and watch the snow?"

"I feel weird," she said with a sigh, running her fingers through her damp hair. "I mean, what was I supposed to do? Walk in there and say, okay, here I am, go ahead and spank me."

"Sure, that'd be fine."

"No, Liam, that would be weird."

"Have you changed your mind?"

"It's not that I've changed my mind, it's that I'm....I don't know what I am," she muttered, shaking her head.

"You're feelin' embarrassed, but that's natural."

"I guess."

"Summer, if you wanna back out, no problem."

Taking a breath, she stared out at the wild snow. He might break her heart, but it was worth a roll of the dice, and she knew she'd kick herself if she didn't at least give him a shot.

She realized she was kidding herself.

There was no choice.

Her feelings for him were too strong.

She couldn't walk away even if she wanted to.

"I think," she said softly, turning away from the window and staring up at him, "I need another kiss."

"If I kiss you, the next thing I'll do is take you to that couch and put you over my knee."

"Good grief."

"Do you want me to kiss you?"

"Uh-huh."

"Are you sure?"

"Uh-huh."

Though the simple acknowledgement was all she could manage, Summer had never been so sure of anything in her life, but he'd been right when he'd suggested she was embarrassed. She didn't have butterflies fluttering in her stomach, she had gymnasts doing tumbling routines. Her heart raced, and she was breathless at just the thought of being stretched over his lap.

He gripped her arms.

He leaned his head down.

Closing her eyes as his mouth pressed against hers, she sank into the kiss. His lips glided, the tip of his tongue teased, and as he became more aggressive, she was sure her legs would buckle.

"You ready for your spankin'?" he whispered, moving his mouth to her ear. "You want it real bad, don't you, sugar?"

"I do," she managed. "I don't know why, but I do."

Moving his arm around her waist, he guided her to the couch, sat down, then quickly pulled her across his thighs.

"How long will this last?" she mewled, looking at him over her shoulder.

"You'll find out," he said, smoothing his hand over her full, round backside. "Are you ready?"

"I guess."

"Try again. Are you ready?"

"Yes."

* * *

He knew his smacks wouldn't have much of an impact over the thick velvet of the sweat pants, but he wasn't ready to pull them down. Knowing any protests would be contrived, he began to spank. As he carried his hand from cheek to cheek, she stayed still, letting out an occasional ouch or an ow, but he didn't care about the minor ejaculations of pain.

He'd achieved his goal.

She was beginning to relax.

As she let out a sigh, a slight smile curled the edges of his lips. He recognized the sigh hadn't been one of relief, but of disappointment.

It was time.

He slid his fingers under the elastic waistband.

"Liam! What are you doing?"

"What do you think I'm doin'?" he drawled, slowly pushing the pants over her luscious globes.

"No! You didn't say anything about making me naked!"

"You want me to stop?"

He'd only moved them a few inches, but he paused, waiting for her answer.

"I, uh…"

"It's a yes or no question."

"I, uh…"

"You said that already. I'm not gonna sit here all day. Yes or no?"

"Oh, God…yes."

Though her voice had been a squeak, it had been clear. He continued, but a second later he discovered she was wearing no panties.

"Aren't you a naughty girl?"

"Are you complaining?" she shot back.

His hand blasted down with a hot smack.

"Ow!"

"You really wanna be sassy right now?"

"That hurt!"

"Yep, and it's gonna hurt again," he declared, landing another.

"Fuck!"

"You go ahead and cuss if you want, it's not gonna change how I'm gonna spank you, though I might add a few more. Swearin' like a trooper doesn't look good on you, sugar."

Before she could respond, he flattened his palm and began slapping with gusto. Her wriggling and protests fell on deaf ears, and when she began kicking out, he calmly moved one of his legs over the back of her knees.

"Summer," he said patiently, pausing his hand.

"What?" she panted. "Damn, my ass is stinging."

"And why do you think that is?"

"Because you've been spanking me!"

"Hmm, let me rephrase. Why have I been spankin' you?"

He heard the sharp intake of breath.

Her brain had clicked in.

"Because I lied to you."

"Keep goin'."

"Because I lied to you and kept lying to you for three months."

"You think your butt is hot enough for what you did?"

It was a question he often asked. Though he determined the discipline, the female over his lap knew the extent of her guilt and shame.

"Yes, it hurts," she whimpered, "but, uh..."

"But what? Tell me, Summer."

"The accident. I should've put my car into four-wheel drive, and I should never have been fooling with my bag. Now my car's probably totaled and I hate myself. I was an idiot."

"Yes you were, and you'll get ten hard smacks on each side, but not on your red ass," he declared, pushing her pants to her knees. "They're goin' right here, right where you sit."

She wriggled and let out a groan, but not from his warning. She knew her pussy was now open to his eye, and she yearned to feel his touch. As his hand began moving back and forth where her thighs met her bottom, she couldn't stop the long, aching need escaping her lips.

"Are you ready, Summer?"

His stern voice snapped her from her salacious thoughts, but his hand rested tantalizingly close to her sex. Hoping to tempt him, she opened her legs as much as the sweat pants around her knees would allow.

"Don't make me ask again," he scolded, ignoring the invitation.

"Yes, I'm ready," she said with a resigned sigh, not surprised her subtle attempt at seduction had been unsuccessful.

The first slap landed. She bit her lower lip ready for the next, but he made her wait, then delivered the second on the same spot. Again he paused, then inflicted the third on top of the first two.

"Ow, oh, that stings," she yelled, squirming on his lap.

"That's the point," he declared, landing the next. "That accident was completely preventable. You could've been badly injured, or worse. This

is the least you deserve," he scolded, whisking his palm over her stinging sit spot, evoking a loud howl.

"Please, Liam, I'll be more careful in future. I will. I swear."

"I believe you, but that promise won't get you out of the rest of your
punishment."

The next slap was harder, and she yelped loudly, then stared at him
over her shoulder.

"Liam, please," she sniffled, "I'm really—"

But she was cut off mid-sentence with the next stinging blow, then
to her shock, he landed the last three swiftly, scorching her skin and
taking her breath away.

"Those were for not puttin' your car in four-wheel drive," he exclaimed. "The other side will pay for messin' with your bag when you
should've been focused on your drivin'."

"Ooh, yes, Sir."

Liam raised his eyebrows.

She had called him Sir.

It had slipped from her lips as naturally as breathing. He had an instinct for recognizing a submissive soul, and he'd been right about her.

"Are you ready, young lady?"

"Yes, Sir."

"These will be no different. The first seven slow, the last three quick.
Yell all you want, but it won't stop me," he said sternly, landing the first.

"Ow!"

"Ask for the next one."

"What?" she gasped, sure she must have misunderstood.

"You heard me, and don't make me repeat myself."

"I, uh, oh, Sir, please spank me?"

"I certainly will," he replied, flicking down his flattened palm, eliciting a sharp cry. "Ask again, Summer, but add the word harder."

She uttered a surprised cry, but she had to obey him, and she wanted to.

"Please, Sir, spank me harder?" she bleated, wondering if there was something wrong with her as the smack landed with a fiery sting.

"Once more."

"Ooh, please Sir, spank me harder?"

The spicy slap was quickly administered.

He paused.

"I'm waiting."

"Please spank me harder."

"You forgot the sir. Do that again and I'll add another."

"Oh, please, Sir, spank me harder?"

Though the sharp, hot swat made her squeal and kick, she immediately requested the next. It kissed her burning skin with more scalding heat, and was quickly followed with the remaining three. Panting and sniffling, she writhed in his lap, then moaned piteously as he began to rub away the prickling pain.

"Have you been punished enough for the accident?"

"Yes, I have," she whimpered. "I'll never be so stupid again. I swear."

"Take a deep breath and let it out. I'm gonna rub you for a minute."

She sucked in the air, slowly exhaled, then sank into his lap as she surrendered to his soothing caress.

Silent minutes ticked by.

"How're you feelin', sugar?" he finally asked, his voice no longer stern, but soft and tender.

"It's weird," she said softly, "but I feel better. Different, somehow."

"Sit up and curl into my lap."

His invitation washed over her like a warm blanket, and not caring that her sweat pants were still around her knees, she squirmed her way into his waiting arms.

"There you go," he purred, "punished and forgiven."

"What happens now?" she asked, lifting her eyes to meet his.

"In a few minutes we're going up to my room. You've had a traumatic mornin', and you need a nap."

Her brow furrowed in disappointment.

"You just have to be patient Summer Brown. I expect that's not easy for you, but I'll be helpin' you with that as well."

CHAPTER SIX

Summer blinked open her eyes. The room was in semi-darkness, the only light coming from the soft amber glow of the fire. She couldn't remember ever having slept so deeply, but as she rolled over to snuggle against Liam, she was dismayed to find the bed empty. Sitting up and stretching, she let out a long yawn, then glanced across at the clock on the nightstand. 6:37 p.m. She'd slept the entire afternoon.

Slipping from the sheets, she padded over to her clothes lying on a nearby chair. Quickly dressing, she spied a partially open door leading into Liam's bathroom. Ambling in, she found herself staring at Carrera marble, a huge shower stall, and a large jacuzzi tub. It was another reminder of Liam Taylor's wealth. She felt a sudden wave of insecurity.

Pushing it aside, she ran a comb through her hair, splashed her face with warm water, then hurried from the bedroom and made her way down the stairs in search of him. Though she could still hear the blizzard raging outside, it was overshadowed by the soulful voice of one of Liam's famous artists, Suzann DeMure. Liam had discovered her in an underground club in New Orleans. Summer felt a pang of envy.

Why hadn't she been discovered?

Why wouldn't Liam at least listen to her?

Telling herself not to think about it, she headed down the hall to his den, but as she walked in she stopped short. He was standing at his desk over his open briefcase and holding her phone.

"Liam! What the hell?"

"Excuse me?" he asked, frowning across at her.

"My phone!"

"What about it?"

"Why do you have it?" she asked brusquely, striding across to him. "Are you—"

"Am I what," he interrupted. "Scrollin' through your emails and messages? Is that what you're askin' me?"

33

Though irritation flashed from his eyes, his voice had been chillingly calm.

"Why else would you have it?"

Wordlessly he dropped it back in his briefcase, clicked the locks shut, then quickly stepping up to her, he grabbed her wrists and pinned them behind her back.

"You listen to me real good, sugar. I would no more snoop through your phone than I would go joggin' in that blizzard outside."

"I, uh..."

"Hush up! You left it here. I'd put it in my case to take to the airfield and give it to the manager so you'd—"

"I'm sorry, I didn't know," she said hastily, silently cursing herself for jumping to such an ugly conclusion.

"I told you to hush up," he scolded. "Don't interrupt me again."

"Sorry."

"I'd forgotten all about it until I opened my case just now. When I noticed the cover, I thought about gettin' one like it for my sister. That's why I was lookin' at it. I'm not the kinda guy that would look through your personal stuff. You got that? If I wanna know somethin' I'll ask. Are we clear?"

"Yes, sorry."

Dropping her wrists, he immediately wrapped her into his arms.

"How's your butt?" he asked, smoothing his hands over her backside.

"A bit tender."

"You pull that crap with me again and I'll freshen it up real quick."

"I won't."

"Are you hungry?"

"I hadn't thought about it but, now that you mention it, yes, I am."

"Come into the kitchen," he said, releasing her and taking her hand. "I'll rustle us up somethin' to eat."

"Um, what about my phone?"

"You'll get it back when you've settled down."

"What? Liam, I am settled, and I'm not ten years old!"

"You sure as hell are, sugar," he said softly, pausing his step and looking down at her. "I told you, I'm different."

"I know, but—"

"But nothin'. The punishment should fit the crime. It does, and now you're poutin' about it."

"I am not."

"Yeah, you are," he retorted with a wink. "Now let's eat. I've been waitin' for you and I'm starvin'."

But as she fell into step beside him, he could sense she was still upset. He'd scolded her like a child and taken away her phone. Her indignation was understandable. She obviously wasn't used to having an authority figure.

"Whatta you in the mood for?" he asked as they entered the gourmet kitchen. "Soup, pasta, scrambled eggs?"

"Whatever."

"Whatever? I'm not sure I have any whatever. I'll cook us up some pasta."

"I should see if my parents emailed me."

"Yeah, you probably should."

"I'll be back in a minute."

As she ambled away, he shook his head—but he also grinned. She was a brat, but that was fine with him, and their chemistry was undeniable. He knew she'd try to open his briefcase, and when she couldn't it would tick her off even more. Was he being high-handed? Probably, but he needed to start things off on the right foot or there'd be trouble ahead.

"What am I thinkin'?" he muttered. "With that girl, there's trouble ahead regardless."

* * *

Entering his den, Summer walked briskly across to his briefcase and tried to pop it open. It was locked. She cursed under her breath. She would have put the cellphone back, but she wanted to see if there were any texts or voicemails. Sandy, her best friend, always had such great words of wisdom, and she might have left a message before the cell service went down.

She'd been talking to Sandy when Liam had overheard the incriminating conversation. For the umpteenth time she had insisted Summer tell him the truth, and Summer had made the comment about singing all morning to no avail.

"Dammit," she muttered, staring at the briefcase. "I guess it doesn't matter. It's all out in the open now anyway."

Moving behind the desk and powering up the computer, she logged into her account and found two emails waiting for her. The first was from her father, the second from Sandy. She'd be able to read her best friend's pearls of wisdom after all, but she opened her father's email first.

Sweetheart, your mother and I are so relieved you weren't hurt in the accident. Don't worry, we'll take care of the car once the storm is passed. We wish you were here to celebrate Christmas Eve, but knowing you're safe is the most important thing. We'll be able to Skype a bit later. We'll be going next door for drinks, assuming we can walk across the yard in the blizzard. I'll try you on Skype when we get back. It shouldn't be too late. Let me know you got this. Love you, Dad.

Relieved and happy, she sent back a quick response wishing them a fun time, and promised to check the computer later that night, then opened the email from Sandy.

Hey, Summer. I heard Liam's voice right before the call ended. I guess the cat's out of the bag. It's about time. You know how I think you should have told him why you were really there since day one. I don't know what's happening between you two right now, but I

hope everything's okay. **Just be straight with him, and don't pull any of your bratty pouty crap. That won't help anything. Love you. Sandy.**

"My bratty pouty crap," Summer muttered. "Shit."

She quickly typed her response.

Sandy, I'm so glad to hear from you. I had a car accident on the way home after our conversation, but Liam found me. He got me out of the storm and brought me back to his house. Things are amazing, but you're right. I need to do exactly what you said. You're always my voice of reason. Thank you so much. Love you back. Summer.

Hitting SEND, she logged out, but Sandy's words stayed with her as she walked back to the kitchen

Don't pull any of your bratty pouty crap.

To her chagrin, Summer knew she'd done just that.

"I take it there was an email from your folks," he remarked as she entered. "I'll bet they were happy to hear from you."

"Totally," she replied with a big smile. "What can I do to help?"

"You look better."

"I got an email from a friend of mine as well."

"The one you were talking to earlier?"

"Yeah, that one, and I'm sorry I got all weird about my phone. I totally overreacted."

He'd been stirring the pasta, and placing the wooden spoon on the counter, he moved across to her, held her face in his hands and softly kissed her.

"You're forgiven, but next time..."

"There won't be a next time."

"Of course there will. Brats aren't exorcised in a day."

"Am I really a brat?"

"You can certainly act like one, and as long as you're with me, when you do there'll be consequences."

"You mean you'll spank me?"

"Maybe, maybe not. Just know you'll pay a price."

Her butterflies had started up again, and dropping her head into his shoulder, she wrapped her arms around his waist. She'd been crazy about him for weeks, but now she was falling deep.

"I was thinkin', it's Christmas Eve," he continued. "Why don't we have dinner by candlelight?"

"Here in the kitchen?"

"Somewhere much cozier. In front of the fire in the livin' room."

"That sounds heavenly, but with the fire going, will we still need candles?"

"We will definitely need candles. There are some in that cabinet by the nook. Grab two of the tall ones marked soy wax, and there'll be a red and white checked tablecloth in the drawer just below it."

"Soy wax? I've never heard of soy wax candles."

"You have now, and once you've used them, you'll never want to burn anything else."

"Huh, that sounds interesting," she said happily, then pulling back she gazed into his twinkling brown eyes. "Thanks, Liam."

"For what?"

"Putting up with me. I know I can be a bit difficult."

"I have no problem with difficult. I kinda like it. Now let me go, woman, I need to check the pasta."

"Yes, Sir," she said with a giggle.

Walking across to the cabinet, she found the candles and the tablecloth, and carried them into the living room. As she started moving the books and various bits and pieces from the coffee table to a nearby bookshelf, a warm chill of excitement rippled through her body. If she couldn't spend Christmas Eve with her family, there was nowhere else she'd rather be, than exactly where she was.

CHAPTER SEVEN

With the fire flaming and the candles softly flickering, Liam and Summer were sitting on the floor with their backs against the couch. Sharing Christmas stories as they ate the perfectly cooked linguini, she took her last bite and declared the spicy tomato sauce was the best she'd ever tasted.

"I'm glad you like it. I've never found anythin' better. It came all the way from a family restaurant in Little Italy."

"Little Italy, New York?"

"Yep. It's made in their kitchen by the grand matriarch. I swear she's a hundred-years-old, and she rules that place like a mafia Don."

"No wonder it tastes so good."

The smooth bottle of Napa Valley cabernet was almost empty, and he shared the last of it between them.

"To you," he said, raising his glass. "A beautiful but naughty girl who has made this Christmas Eve one I'll never forget."

"And to you, Liam," she declared. "This will be a Christmas Eve I'll never forget too—not ever!"

They clinked and drank.

Tilting his head to the side and studying her for a moment, he placed his glass on the table, and taking hers from her hand, he set it down, then leaned in and languidly kissed her. Though it began softly, the kiss took fire, leaving them breathless when they finally broke apart.

"I have more planned for this evening," he murmured, carrying his mouth to her neck.

"You do?" she panted, surrendering to the delicious goosebumps caused by his warm tongue trailing across her skin.

"Do you like surprises?" he asked, raising his head and gazing into her eyes.

"I definitely like surprises."

"Do you trust me?"

"Absolutely."

"I'm gonna blindfold you."

"Ooh, Liam, I would love that," she mewled, pressing her body against him, but his fingers suddenly fisted her hair and tugged it back.

"I'm leavin', but I'll only be a minute. When I come back I wanna find you naked."

"Liam, you turn me on so much. I'd say so fucking much, but you don't like it when I swear."

"There are exceptions, and that's one of them."

As he released her hair, she wished he'd clutched it even tighter and consumed her mouth with another greedy kiss. Watching him rise to his feet, pick up their plates and walk away, she closed her eyes and took a long breath. Liam Taylor was the sexiest man on the planet, and he was absolutely, positively, stealing her heart.

Buzzed from the wine, she removed her clothes and stayed sitting on the floor. It felt odd to be naked, but she was abruptly distracted by a rich, deep voice crooning a bluesy love song. Hearing Liam's approach, she turned to see him moving towards her wearing a black cotton robe.

"Who is that singing?" she asked as he sat on the couch behind her.

"My next superstar. His name is David McDaniel. His first CD comes out a week before Valentine's Day."

"He's incredible. His voice is like that wine we just drank. Smooth and velvety."

"Hmmm. I might use that. Drink in the voice of David McDaniel. Yep, I like it a lot. I'll shoot it over to my PR team."

"Really?"

"Really, but right now I'm focused on you. Close your eyes, my beautiful, naked girl."

"You mean I'm not naughty anymore?" she quipped. "Just beautiful and naked?"

"You're all three. A beautiful, naked, naughty girl who needs to do as she's told."

"Yes, Sir."

"Have you ever called anyone sir before?"

"No, never, it just sort of came out. I love how it makes me feel when I say it."

Liam felt an unfamiliar surge of emotion.

Too many times he'd experienced the insincerity of a woman pretending to be turned on when she wasn't. Summer might have lied her way into his house, but there was nothing phony about her submissive responses.

"Makes you feel, how?" he pressed. "Be specific."

"Um," she murmured thoughtfully. "The best word I can think of is gooey. Like hot caramel."

"That's what you are, hot caramel with a hint of cayenne pepper," he whispered, his lips warm against her ear as he fondled her breasts "and I'm gonna eat you up, but first you've gotta lie on the floor and spread your legs. I wanna watch you play with your pussy."

"Can't we sit here for just a minute longer?" she whimpered, lost in his fervent fondling.

"You will, but I'm steppin' away for a minute."

"No," she bleated, grabbing one of his wrists. "I refuse to let you go."

"Is that right?"

"Yes, that's right!"

"You're' bein' naughty!"

"Maybe, but—ouch," she squealed as he sharply pinched a nipple.

"That should keep you company for the few seconds I'm gone."

"Ow. Was that really necessary?"

"Yep, and you are really pushing your luck," he scolded, though wearing a grin she couldn't see. "Just stay there, and no more back-talk."

As she felt him rise off the couch and move away, she wondered what other salacious surprises he might have in store, and though she strained to listen, she couldn't interpret any of the sounds she heard.

"I've moved the coffee table out of the way," he declared. "Get on all fours and crawl forward. You'll feel a rug."

It was surreal, moving across the floor blindfolded and naked, but she loved it, and when she felt the fur under her hands, she couldn't wait to lie in its warm, fuzzy softness.

"I've gotta tell you, Summer, you sure look good on your hands and knees, especially with that gorgeous backside so lovely and pink. You know I'm gonna be spankin' you more often than not."

"You are, Sir? Why?"

"I have a sayin'. A spankin' a day keeps the brat away."

"Am I a brat?"

"You sure as hell can be, and as much as I'd like to keep lookin' at you just as you are, it's time to lie on your back."

Her butterflies fluttering, she did as he instructed, and placing her fingers against her clit, she began the erotic massage.

"That's a mighty nice picture," he crooned. "Leg's wider.. Imagine you're in your bed with my T-shirt."

Her surprised gasp made him chuckle, but her hand nestled against her sex had stopped rubbing. Bending down, he sharply slapped the inside of each thigh.

"Ooh, Sir," she wailed. "Ooh..."

"I didn't give you permission to hit the pause button," he scolded. "Disobedience has consequences."

"I'm sorry, Sir. I was just so shocked you knew about me taking your T-shirt."

"I was pleased you did. It told me how you were feelin' about me, but right now you'd better start playin' with yourself again. Like I said, do it just the way you do when you're alone and thinkin' about me. Is the shirt usually next to you?"

"No, Sir."

"Tell me where you usually have it."

"It's a bit embarrassing, Sir."

"I can slap your thighs 'til you stop feelin' that way."

"No, no," she said quickly. "I lay it over my face."

"Almost like your own blindfold. Aren't you clever? Tell me one of the things you've imagined over the last month."

"Uh...my back's against a wall," she began breathlessly, "and you're holding my wrists in one of your hands above my head and—and—"

"And...? Don't stop there, sugar."

"Your other hand is under my skirt inside my panties, and your mouth, it's devouring my neck like a vampire. Ooh, Sir."

"Keep goin'."

"Then you turn me around—and—ooh—you tell me to keep my arms where they are, then you lift my skirt and slap me, then tease between my legs, then slap me again, and you keep doing that until I..."

"Until you come, just like you're real close to doin' right now?"

"Yes, yes."

"Stop!"

"Oh, Sir, please, I can't. I need to keep going!"

"Bad girl!" he growled, grabbing her wrist and jerking her hand away. "You'll have to be punished for that. Put both hands at your side and throw your legs over your head."

"Sir? Over my head?"

"Wow, you must really wanna get your butt whipped."

"No, no, sorry," she panted urgently, swinging her legs in the air.

As she bent them over her head, she suddenly felt the lewd exposure. Her faced burned hot, but the humiliation was quickly forgotten as he began swatting her bottom.

"Ow, ow, I'm sorry!"

"You're gonna learn, sugar," he declared, pausing for a moment. "I warned you more than once, but I reckon testin' is in your nature."

"I'm sorry. I'll behave, I will."

"Your pussy sure is wet," he muttered, pushing his finger into her slit. "Man, you are soaked."

Summer was overwhelmed.

His finger twirled around her clit, then moved in and out of her in a torturous tease. On top of that, her backside was stinging, she was lewdly exposed, and her pussy was yearning for his cock. It was so much more than she'd ever expected, but she loved every second, and she never wanted it to end.

"Lower your legs, and next time I tell you to stop you'd best do it. Clear?"

"Yes, Sir," she whimpered. "Very clear. Crystal clear."

Her legs sank back into the soft fur, and she was about to touch herself again when she realized he hadn't asked her to. She waited, determined not to do anything without a specific instruction.

"Put your hands behind your head and keep them there. You're gonna feel somethin' hot land on your skin, but it'll only burn for a second or two."

"Yes, Sir," she replied, locking her fingers together behind her head. "Sir, may I ask a question?"

"Yeah?"

"I'm a bit scared."

"Good, that means your adrenalin's pumpin'. Are you ready?"

"Eek, yes, I'm ready."

"Did you just say eek?"

"Uh-huh."

He stifled a chuckle. Summer was a kick, but he needed to concentrate.

Picking up one of the tall, glass candles, he held it above her body, then carefully let a dollop of wax fall on her stomach. She yelped, but as the wax cooled and solidified, a soft moan left her lips.

"Again?"

"I'm not sure. Ooh, it's kind of amazing. Uh, yes, Sir."

He dribbled more below each of her breasts.

She gasped, then mewled.

She was surrendering to the pain/pleasure seesaw.

"More?"

"I'd love more, Sir."

"A trail this time, then you'll put your fingers back against your clit. Are you ready?"

"A trail? Ooh, yes, Sir."

Spilling the wax on her chest, he carried it between her breasts and down to her belly button. Though she was panting, he spotted her thighs tense and release as the wax congealed. Placing the candle back on the coffee table, he touched between her legs.

"Damn, girl, you're drenched. Put your fingers on your pussy and tell me another T-shirt story."

"I'm naked," she murmured as her hand moved against her sex, "but you're dressed in a dark suit and white shirt. You're sitting behind a desk and I'm next to you, bent over it."

"I'm likin' this," he growled, quickly removing his robe and straddling her body. "Keep goin'."

"You're working, but every so often you reach between my legs and play with me and pinch my ass, then say things like, no, not wet enough yet—ooh, Sir, I'm so hot."

"When you're ready you can come. Say thank you, and thank you again after your orgasm."

"Yes, Sir, thank you, Sir."

"Keep talkin'," he ordered, taking hold of his cock and fervently stroking. "You're over my desk and I'm teasin' your pussy. Then what?"

"I hear you stand up, then you're behind me telling me to arch my back."

"I'm takin' over," he said huskily. "I start spankin' your ass and checkin' your wetness..."

"Ooh, yes, Sir, ooh, I'm so close."

"I unzip my fly and pull out my cock."

"I'm almost there."

"And grabbin' your hips, I thrust inside you..."

"Sir, I'm coming!"

Watching her puckered nipples, and the deep orgasmic blush cross her chest, he spewed his essence across her breasts. It was a strong, satisfying climax, but she was still in the throes of her orgasm. Listening to her short, sharp cries, he quickly dropped to her side and sent his lips against her ear.

"Keep it goin', sugar, that's my girl, keep it goin'."

Letting out a wail, she pushed herself into more, and turning his head to gaze down the length of her body, he spied her thighs urgently pressing together. Images of her legs tied wide apart danced in his head, and moments later, with a long, heavy, whimpered thank you, Sir, she fell limp.

Kissing her softly, he rose to his feet, pulled on his robe, and walked briskly to the powder room in the hall. He needed to fetch a damp towel to clean her up, then he'd have the pleasure of peeling off the wax.

Normally he wouldn't introduce candle play until he'd been seeing someone for a while, but his instinct had told him she'd love it.

He'd been right.

Summer Brown was a passionate and wonderfully challenging submissive.

But there was the issue of her ambition.

Would it get in the way?

CHAPTER EIGHT

After Liam languidly peeled the wax from Summer's body, they dressed and washed the dishes together, but after sleeping through the afternoon neither felt ready to go upstairs to bed. Crossing his arms and leaning back against the kitchen counter, Liam tilted his head and stared at her.

"What?" she asked, walking over to him, intrigued by the look in his impenetrable milk-chocolate eyes.

"I'm just thinkin'."

"That's obvious. Thinking about what?"

"Takin' you down and showin' you the studio."

"Seriously? Well you have to now,!" she said vehemently. "You can't drop a bombshell like that and not do it."

In the three months she'd worked for him, she'd never been through the locked door at the end of the hall. The recording studio had been strictly off-limits.

"Yeah, I guess maybe you're right about that."

"I am! Will you take me there now?"

"Have you ever been in a studio?"

"Only in my dreams," she replied sheepishly. "I guess that's kind of embarrassing for a girl who claims to be a singer."

"You'd be surprised how many talented people doin' the club scene in Nashville would say the same. David McDaniel had never been in one 'til I found him."

"I'm glad you told me that. Thank you."

"You've gotta promise not to touch anything."

"You don't have to worry about that. I'd be afraid to."

"Good answer," he said with a grin.

"I meant, I'd be worried about pushing a wrong button and screwing something up!"

"Of course you did," he said with a chuckle, taking her hand. "It used to be the basement. The minute I walked down there I knew it would be perfect," he continued, leading her from the kitchen and down the hall.

Stopping at the door, he entered the combination on the metal key-pad and pushed it open.

Her heart began to race.

She was about to enter Liam Taylor's inner sanctum.

The place where the magic happened.

With a theatrical wave of his arm, he ushered her forward.

As she walked down the thickly carpeted stairs, her eyes grew wide. The recording studio looked like every picture she'd ever seen, except bigger and better.

"This is amazing," she muttered, a rush of energy pulsing through her body.

"Come into the control booth. I'll show you the equipment."

Following him inside, she stared into the space where the singers sang and the musicians played.

Her vision flashed through her head.

Then a wave of nerves.

Big stars recorded there.

Would she measure up?

"Summer?"

"Who's been here?" she managed. "I mean, have you done much recording?"

"I didn't spend a fortune putting in all this equipment for fun, but I've only done one album. I haven't been here very long. I built it for my new artists, at least their first CD. The environment is relaxed. They can stay in the house and come down in the middle of the night if inspiration hits them. Summer? Are you okay?"

"Yes, fine."

She'd lied.

Summer was far from okay. .

She was a small-town girl like thousands of other small-town girls who thought they could sing, but she'd had the vision! It had been real! Why was she suddenly so full of self-doubt?

"Are you sure?" he pressed. "You don't look okay."

"Yes, yes, it's just a lot to take in. What's it like?"

"Recording?"

"Uh-huh. I mean, what's typical?"

"There's no such thing. Sometimes we lay down a track and we have to do all kinds of crap to make it sound the way we want. Other times it's a breeze. One of my singers, and I won't tell you who it is, but she has trouble singing parts separately."

"What does that mean?"

"She can sing the whole song and sound great, but if we need to fix certain phrases she has a tough time."

"Oh. I see. I've never done anything like that," she said quietly, and as she peered through the glass, in spite of her premonition, she wondered if she'd ever get the chance.

* * *

Liam had been watching Summer closely. He hadn't brought her into his studio just so she could see it. He'd wanted to gauge her reaction, and she suddenly seemed more intimidated than excited. The reality of performing in a professional setting had hit her, and it was daunting.

"Would you like to go in there?" he asked, pointing through the glass.

"Um, yeah."

"You don't have to. I just thought you'd like to."

"I do, but I'm confused."

"About what?"

"You made it clear being with you had to stay strictly personal, and I wasn't to get any ideas about singing, but now you've brought me here."

"Would you have preferred not to see it?"

"No, no, I'm excited to see it."

"This wasn't meant as a big tease," he murmured with a frown. "I'm sorry. Maybe it was a mistake."

"No, please don't say that. I'm really grateful, more than you know. The truth is, being in here is kind of like a wake-up call. I've had fantasies about becoming a star, but now I don't know if I'm good enough. Is that why you brought me down here? So I'd get that? It is, isn't it?"

"That's part of it," he said gently, putting an arm around her shoulders. "Summer, singin' for your supper isn't just openin' your mouth and carryin' a tune. It takes a whole lotta work, and a unique voice with an unforgettable quality, that's rare."

"I'm feeling really strange right now."

"I didn't mean to upset you," he said, wrapping her up and hugging her tightly, "but there's another reason I wanted you to see this place. This is my life. I spend hours upon hours down here, and when I'm workin' with an artist I'm consumed."

"You should be, you would have to be," she said earnestly, pulling back and looking up at him. "How can you make something perfect if you're not obsessed? The only way to make something great is to live it, breathe it, have it rolling around in your head every waking second. Of course you'd be consumed."

Her solemn, profound response startled him. She'd sounded older and wiser than the sexy, bubbly Summer he'd come to know.

"I'm not wrong," she added, misunderstanding his silence. "You may think I—"

"No, you're not! I'm just surprised you understand. I mean, really understand."

"It's how I am when..."

"When?"

"You don't want to know," she murmured, turning away and gazing through the glass at the empty room.

"Of course I want to know, tell me."

"It's how I am when I'm writing a song. The words, the melody, they live in my head. I can't think about anything else until it's finished. It drives my mother batty sometimes."

Liam's heart skipped.

Her smoky speaking voice suggested she could probably sing, and was she more than just another pretty girl who had a modicum of talent and big dreams?

"Will you bring me down here again?" she asked, turning back to look at him.

"Sure."

"Maybe I won't feel so strange next time."

"I can help with that right now."

Placing his hands on either side of her face, he leaned in and brushed her lips with his. He'd meant the kiss to be warm and reassuring, but she raised her arms around his neck and fervently kissed him back.

"Will you hold me all night?" she breathed as she broke away. "I need you to."

"Try and stop me."

"I'm glad you brought me down here. Thank you."

"You are?"

"Yeah, I am. Truly."

He kissed her again, his hands slid down her back to cup her backside, and as she pressed her pelvis against him, in spite of their shenanigans in the living room, his cock stirred to life.

"Please will you make love to me?" she pleaded. "Right here, right now?"

He'd never had sex in the studio, and it felt right, surprisingly right, but he had no condoms. His mind jumped to the powder room in the hall. He kept a supply there for visiting musicians.

"I'll be right back, but while I'm gone strip off and lie on the floor. I wanna walk in and see you naked just like before."

"Not the couch over there?" she asked, waving at a long leather chesterfield against the wall.

"Nope, on the floor," he muttered, and quickly releasing her, he hurried out the door.

As he trotted up the stairs he had only one thought. Finding a condom and finding it fast. Moving swiftly down the hall and entering the small bathroom, he retrieved the packet at the back of the cabinet and grabbed a couple, then snatched up the box of tissues on the counter.Returning briskly back to the sound booth, he entered finding her naked, spread eagled and waiting for him. Quickly stripping, he stretched out next to her.

"What took you so long?" she asked with a wink. "I thought you'd gotten lost."

"Are you lookin' for another spankin'?"

She answered by suddenly pressing her body against him and grinding herself against his crotch. Quickly gripping her wrists, he pinned them together above her head with one hand, and dove his mouth to her breasts. Sucking and lapping, he shoved two fingers of his free hand into her soaked channel.

"Fuck, you're wet," he growled, raising his head.

"Liam, I want you," she gasped breathlessly. "I want you right this second."

Releasing her wrists and kneeling between her legs, he sheathed his member, placed himself at her entrance, gripped her hips, and plunged home. As her cry of gratitude echoed through the small chamber, he fell forward, stifling her wail with a rough, crushing kiss, then pulled back just as quickly.

"Damn, girl, I'm gonna fuck you into next week."

"Do it."

As a flicker of challenge danced in her eyes, he straightened up, carefully withdrew, then flipping her on to her stomach, he clutched her waist and jerked her into his pelvis.

"Are you sure?" he growled, placing himself at her entrance.

"Yes."

"Yes, what?"

"Yes, Sir."

He thrust inside her, but didn't move. Staying buried, he landed his flattened palm on her upturned backside with a volley of hot slaps. Gasping and yelping, she looked over her shoulder and stared at him with wide eyes.

"Sir! Ravage me! Please!"

Her urgent plea sent his blood pumping.

Tightening his hands, he slowly withdrew his cock, then pitched back in. Throwing back her head and letting out a cry, he repeated the strong, powerful strokes. He was in control, his cock was consuming her, and feasting his eyes on her freshly reddened ass, he began to accelerate. Her moans filled the room urging him on, and though he vigorously pummeled her pussy, he frequently paused, darting a hand beneath her to tease her clit.

Long minutes of the tantalizing torture continued.

Her cries of pleasure grew louder.

"I'm so close," she finally bleated, her fingers curling into fists.

He paused.

"Sir, please...?"

"No," he said sternly, spanking her with gusto, but stopped as abruptly as he'd started.

Waiting until she'd settled, he resumed his robust thrusts, but as he quickened his pace, he could feel the shadow of his own climax. Slow-ing down, he slipped his fingers beneath her again, found her clit, and urgently rubbed.

"Sir, I won't be able to stop."

"You'd better," he warned, continuing to pump with measured strokes.

"But..."

"Beg."

"Ooh, Sir, please let me come?"

"Will you behave?"

"Yes, yes, I swear. I'm so close. I'm—"

He dropped his hand away.

"Next time you need discipline," he murmured, leaning over her to whisper his warning, "I'll make you wait a long, long time. I might not let you come at all. Clear?"

"Yes, Sir," she panted. "Clear. I'll be so good."

Rising up, he landed a few more smacks, then clutched her hips, found the angle he wanted, and began to pump, increasing the pace as his climax grew closer.

"Please, Sir, please may I come?"

"Not yet."

"Now, Sir?" she mewled. "I'm there!"

"No."

She suddenly arched her back.

"Sir..." she pleaded, her voice a high pitched wail.

"On the count of three, and not a second sooner."

"Ooh, yes, Sir. Thank you, Sir."

"One—two—three. Come now! Right now!"

As she let out a fresh howl and bucked back against him, a series of tingling convulsions rippled through his loins. Groaning loudly through each sparkling spasm, he could hear her euphoric cries as she rode the waves of her glorious orgasm. As his last shudder subsided and he slipped out, she fell on her stomach, then rolled on her back.

Though utterly drained, he took a moment to gaze down at the red bloom across her chest before dropping beside her.

"That was amazing," she panted, resting her head in the crook of his shoulder. "Liam, your heart, it's pounding so hard."

"Sure feels like it," he murmured, moving his arms around her, then cloaked in the serenity of the afterglow, they closed their eyes and drifted.

"I guess this studio is christened now," he finally muttered, stirring from the short doze. "I can't believe you talked me into it. I'm protective about this place."

"I did not talk to you into it!"

"You sure made it hard to say no."

"I think I can die a happy woman now."

"Glad to hear it, but you've had enough brushes with death for one day," he remarked, reaching for a tissue and pulling off the condom. "Man, I'm beat."

"Me too. Totally tanked."

"Time for bed."

"I need to see if mom and dad are around," Summer muttered with a sigh. "They told me they'd try to Skype when they got home from the party at the neighbors."

"You do that, sugar," he said as they slowly stood up and began to dress. "I'm gonna hit the hay. Come up whenever. Will you do me a favor and check the weather while you're online?"

"Good idea. I will, for sure."

Slowly climbing the stairs, he walked her down the hall to his den, then paused at the door and brought her into his arms.

"Summer," he began softly, "except for findin' you in a ditch, I wouldn't change this Christmas Eve for a second."

"Me too," she murmured, melting against him, "but even the ditch part is okay. It's what made all this happen."

"I guess you're right about that. See you in a minute. Tell your folks I said hi."

Resting his lips on hers in a long, languid kiss, he ambled away. Starting up the stairs, an odd feeling rumbled through his being.

Summer was special.

CHAPTER NINE

Ambling up the stairs, Summer could feel the fatigue moving through her body. Her muscles ached, and she had a dull throbbing in her head. The low fire flickering in the fireplace welcomed her as she entered the bedroom, and seeing Liam waiting, she let out a grateful sigh. The room was warm and cozy, and she couldn't wait to curl into his arms.

"Hey, you," he murmured with a sleepy smile. "What's the news?"

"Do you want the good news, the good news, or the good news?" she asked, removing her clothes and collapsing into bed.

"I already know some of the good news."

"You do? What?"

"You're in my bed," he replied, wrapping her up, "and that, sugar, is very good news."

"I agree. You should consider yourself extraordinarily lucky."

"Cute, and for the record I do. Now tell me what's happenin'."

"I was able to talk to mom and dad and you are officially invited to Christmas dinner tomorrow, assuming we can get out of here."

"Cool. I'd love to go. Next?"

"The storm is moving out. The nasty stuff ends overnight."

"That's not good news, that's great news. What's the third thing?"

"Oh, actually those are the three things. Talking to mom and dad, you're invited to dinner, and the storm's clearing out."

"Ah, I see."

"Liam, I feel like I've been hit by a bus. I don't think I've ever been this tired, and I feel weird, like, achy."

"You want some aspirin?"

"I found some in the powder room."

"You need a good night's sleep, probably more than one. We'll lounge here in the mornin' and recover."

"Yes please," she muttered, snuggling even closer. "I'm sure you're right. A deep sleep and a lazy morning."

Though she was utterly exhausted and physically drained, Summer was happier than she could ever remember being. With the fire's light cloaking her, and Liam's warm body beside her, she closed her eyes and drifted away.

It wasn't quite daybreak. Standing on the roof of Liam's house, she was cold, as cold as she'd been when she'd been trapped in her car. Gazing up at the mountain's peak she saw the huge white wall moving towards her. There was an eerie whooshing sound, but it was loud, like thunder. She had to escape. Liam had to escape. The mountain was about to fall on top of them.

With a shriek of terror she bolted upright.

Startled from a deep sleep Liam's eyes flew open.

"Hey, Summer, bad dream?" he asked groggily, sitting up and putting his arms around her. "Damn, girl, you're shakin'."

"We have to get out of here. We have to get out of here now!"

"What the hell are you talkin' about?" he asked, switching on the beside lamp.

"There's going to be an avalanche and it's going to hit this house," she said frantically. "We have to get out of here, right now, right this minute."

"Easy, sugar, it was just a nightmare."

"No, no, no, it wasn't. You'll think I'm crazy but...shit...Liam, I have these visions. Not all the time—just—dammit I can't explain this. There's no time. We have to leave."

"Even if this house gets covered in snow we'll be safe until we're dug out," he remarked then realized how ridiculous he'd sounded.

"You don't understand! We have to get out of here right this second!" she exclaimed, her voice filled with panic. "Please, I'm begging you."

"And how are we gonna do that? My Rover can drive through snow, but not when it's real deep, and it's bound to be by now."

"Shit. Let me think, let me think," she muttered, rubbing her forehead. "Skis! Do you have skis? Can you ski?"

"Yeah, I'm a real good skier, but—"

"Listen to me," she said urgently, gripping his upper arms and fixing him with a steady gaze. "This happens to me. Dad has it too. We see things, and I'm telling you, Liam, we must leave. We have to be out of here before daybreak. That's when it's going to happen."

He could see the terror in her eyes, her fingers were digging into his skin, and her voice was filled with barely-controlled panic.

"How do you know it wasn't just a dream?"

"I'm twenty-two years old, Liam. I've had this since the day I was born. I know the difference. We! Must! Leave!"

* * *

Though Liam wasn't completely convinced, he paused for only a moment before letting out a resigned sigh. If there was even the slightest chance Summer had some kind of strange psychic gift and she was right, he had to do as she asked. God forbid he didn't, and they found themselves in the path of a cascading wall of snow.

"Okay, Summer. We'll get outta here. There are skis in the garage. What size shoes do you wear?"

"I'm a seven."

"Thank, God."

"Your sister?"

"Yep. Her ski suits will be in her room."

"Thank you," Summer cried gratefully, throwing her arms around him.

"Let me check how bad it is outside."

Breaking from her arms, he quickly climbed from the bed and hurried across to the windows.

"It's still snowin'" he declared, pulling aside the drapes, "but things have sure calmed down a bunch. Not much wind. Looks like the worst is over, but, uh..."

"What?"

"There's a ton of snow. I hope the gates will open. They should, they're heavy and the motor's strong," he said thoughtfully, then feeling a wave of doubt about her premonition, he turned back to face her. "I've never heard of avalanches in Apple Valley."

"There have been a couple. They were ages ago and they weren't on this mountain, but Liam, I'm right," she said vehemently, then jumping from the bed, she headed for the door. "I'm going to get changed."

Liam's mind was spinning, but as he entered his closet he realized an avalanche wasn't out of the question. The mountain behind the house was steep, and it had been one heck of a storm, probably a record breaker.

"Visions," he muttered as he pulled on his ski suit. "Summer has visions. What the hell?" But his pondering was interrupted when he spotted his knapsack against the back wall. "If we're gonna do this we should have some emergency supplies, and I should take a change of clothes."

Packing hurriedly, he turned off the fire, then walked quickly from the room and down the hall.

"I'm going to grab some provisions in case we get stuck," he called as he walked past his sister's room. "I'll be in the kitchen."

"I'm right behind you," she called back. "I'm looking for goggles."

"Oh, I should have told you. They're in the garage with the poles and skis."

"Okay, I'm coming now."

As she came out of the bedroom he had to smile. She had chosen a suit that was bright pink and trimmed in white fur.

"You look like a snow bunny."

"Thank you, but did you forget we're in dire circumstances? Seconds might count."

"Hey, take a breath. Panickin' isn't gonna help, and you should email your dad," he suggested as they moved down the stairs. "We should be at your house by the time he wakes up, and if we're not he can send out some help."

"That's a great idea."

While Liam moved to the kitchen to stock the backpack, Summer made her way to the den, but when she walked in she felt a wave of sadness.

"I hope this room makes it through," she murmured, gazing at the awards and memorabilia, then powering up the computer and opening her email account, she began to write.

Hi Dad. It's about five-thirty as I write this. An avalanche is going to hit Liam's house. We're leaving on skis. In my vision it was daybreak, so I think we'll get out okay, but I don't know how far past Liam's house the snow will travel. I also don't know how long it will take us to get home, but we'll stay on the main roads. Hopefully we'll run into some snow plows or the sheriff or someone who can pick us up. Just in case something bad happens, I love you and mom more than anything. Btw, now I know what you meant when you told me loving someone special is the most important thing in the world.

I'm sure I'll see you soon.

You're the best dad ever.

Love you heaps.

Summer.

As she hit SEND, she couldn't stop a few stray tears. Taking a breath and wiping them from her face, she rose to her feet, but turning to leave she found Liam waiting for her in the doorway.

"Are you okay?" he asked, walking up to her.

"Yeah, I am. It's just..."

"I know, you're frightened, but hey, the good news is we're gettin' outta here."

"You're right," she nodded, fighting another rush of emotion. "I hope your neighbors will be okay."

"We can't do anything about that, and if you're right, we sure as heck can't stand here talkin' about it." Then pausing he added, "I sure wish I had time to close the shutters."

"We can't risk it," she said as they started down the hall, "and I'm not sure what good they'd do against tons of crashing snow anyway."

"Yeah, you're probably right," he replied, stopping in the kitchen to strap on his knapsack.

Moving into the garage, he opened a stand-up metal cabinet, and standing beside him, she stared in awe at the high-end equipment. She'd skied her whole life, but she'd never used anything like the up-market skis and boots Liam was showing her.

"Holy cow. Are those the new Kastle FX95 HP's?"

"Yep, I just got them about a month ago."

"And Salomons? Dynastars? How often do you ski?"

"As much as I can. Pick your poison."

"For what we'll be doing, um, I guess the Dynastars. What do you think?"

"I agree, and we need headlamps."

A few minutes later he retrieved the garage door remote control from the glove compartment in his SUV. The Rover could operate the door from the rear-view mirror, but Liam made it a point to keep the old-style remote control boxes in case of any glitches. Stuffing it into the front zippered pocket of his jacket for their return, he pushed the button on the wall and waited. Though he could hear the motor above his head trying to crank up the door, it wasn't moving.

"Shit," Liam grunted, hitting the button again to stop it. "The snow must be weighin' it down. I should've checked."

"Now what?"

"The kitchen door. The patio is covered. With any luck the snow hasn't been able to bank up."

"I'm getting scared," she muttered as they moved back inside, carefully carrying their skis and poles. "I hope we get out in time."

"We will. Keep the faith."

Liam opened the kitchen door, but as they stepped outside, they were both shocked by the huge amount of snow.

"Liam! Good grief. How many feet fell? I've never seen anything like it. Have you?"

"I can't say I have, and I've got a bad feelin' about that gate."

"Why?"

"The bars would probably move through it okay, but there's a three foot solid base. I can't see it pushing through all that."

"Not even enough for us to get through?"

"If we go down there and it doesn't work we're screwed. It will take us ages to find another way out?"

"Shit. So, what do we do?"

"Maybe around the side of the house. The wall there is six feet high. From the looks of things the snow could have reached the top."

"You're a genius. That's it, and once we're over it we'll have the protection of the trees in case—"

"Don't even go there," he grimaced, cutting her off, "and I'm not a genius yet. Let's check it out."

The snow was almost as high as the patio, and walking to the steps, they found only the top four were exposed.

"No wonder there could be an avalanche," Liam mumbled as they locked on their skis. "How much frickin' white stuff did we get?"

They pushed off, their headlamps lighting the way, and as they turned the corner of the house, they looked at each other with relieved smiles. The snow was just a couple of feet below the top of the fence. Skiing slowly forward, they found the most advantageous place, and though they had to pull themselves up, the brick wall was wide and easy to maneuver. But the snow on the other side was lower, and they had to jump, but they both landed safely.

"Shit," she exclaimed, "that was hairy."

"We'll be fine now," he said reassuringly. "It's all down hill to the road."

"Liam, you're my hero. You are. You're my superhero. You believed me and you're saving us."

"Hey, you're the one who had the dream. Are you okay? Are you ready to do this?"

"Yes, absolutely, but once we get home you have to hug me for an hour."

"You got it."

Cautiously skiing through the trees, when they finally reached the road they could see the sky lightening over the mountain.

Sunrise!

Unnerved by the approaching daybreak, they attacked the slope, sailing down the winding, snow-covered blacktop. It was eerily silent and still, but their speedy trip made up for the slow pace through the forest. Reaching the bottom of the hill just short of the main road into town, they pulled to a stop, then lifted their goggles to look at the mountain behind them. It was a magnificent sight. A myriad of colors was splashed across the sky, strangely shaped clouds were hovering low, and the jagged peaks looked surreal.

"It's like an oil painting," she said breathlessly. "I've never seen it look like that."

"Are you okay?"

"Yeah, I think so, I just haven't skied in a while and I'm out of shape," she panted, thinking her slight giddiness was due to her huffing and puffing. "At least we're safe now. We can take a minute."

"We're at the bottom of the hill," Liam said gravely. "We might be safe, we might not. It depends on how big the slide is. We should keep goin.'"

"Liam, look," she exclaimed, pointing to the mountain. "What is that?"

"I'm not sure," Liam replied. "There's a pair of binoculars in my backpack. Open the side zipper."

Moving behind him, she opened up the pocket, but as she pulled them out, a wave of dizziness sent her head spinning.

"Here," she said, leaning against him.

"Summer! You're right!" he exclaimed, studying the mountain through the powerful field-glasses. "It's startin'."

"Really?" she muttered, holding his arm waiting for the light-headedness to pass. "Let me see!"

Raising the binoculars to her eyes, the fissure in the snow was plain to see, and what looked like a thin white cloud hovered above it.

"Liam! Oh, my gosh. You're right."

"We need to go," Liam said urgently. "It could travel all the way down, and those things move fast!"

Quickly returning the field glasses in his knapsack, they started off, but her legs were weak, she was having trouble focusing, and suddenly the world began to spin.

"Liam...I...," but before she could finish her legs buckled underneath her and she tumbled to the ground.

"Summer? Summer!"

She could hear his voice, but it was far away, and she had a vague impression of lights. She was being lifted, cocooned in Liam's lap, then everything went black.

CHAPTER TEN

Summer's father padded through the house and into the kitchen to brew some coffee. The house was still asleep, but Keith Brown was used to rising early. Ambling into his den, he powered up his computer to check his email, only to discover an alarming message from his daughter. Picking up the phone and finding no dial tone, he raced back to his bedroom and urgently roused his wife.

"Janet, Janet, get up."

"What? Why? What's wrong?"

"It's Summer. She and Liam Taylor have left his house on skis! They're trying to get back here."

"Why?"

"She had a vision of an avalanche hitting his house."

"No!" Janet exclaimed jumping from the bed. "What should we do?"

"We don't have phone service so I'm gonna get over to the sheriff's office and find Cain. I just hope he's there this early. If anyone can help us he can."

"I'm coming."

"You should stay here with Harry."

"What makes you think I'm gonna stay here?" Harry declared, standing in the open doorway in his pajamas. "You think I'm gonna sit around waitin' to find out what's happened to Summer? Besides, I might be able to help."

"Then get dressed," Janet ordered as she hurried into her closet.

"What? No, I'm goin' by myself!" Keith insisted. "I'm not puttin' either of you in danger."

"You're outvoted dad. I'll be thirty-seconds."

"Why did you do that?" Keith demanded following his wife into the closet.

"Do you honestly think Harry would just sit around here twiddling his thumbs? He'd likely take off in that heap of his and try to find her himself. He's not a little boy anymore, Keith. He's nineteen. There's no way he'd stay put."

"Yeah, I guess you're right."

"Anyway, the storm's passed. There's just a bunch of snow on the ground and we've got the Outback. We'll be okay, but...please tell me our girl's fine."

"Sure she is, honey. She's a great skier. She said they'll be stayin' on the main roads, so if we don't pick them up, one of Cain's deputies will."

Though Keith and Harry had to shovel snow from the front of the garage, they were soon climbing into their Subaru. The snow plows had started clearing the streets, and with the sheriff's office close, it was a quick drive. Turning into the parking lot, they hurriedly left the car and entered the station.

"Is the sheriff in yet? I need to see him right away," Keith said urgently. "It's important."

"There's a lot goin' on right now, sir," the young deputy behind the counter said gravely. "There's been an avalanche."

"I'm here, Keith," his lifelong friend declared, striding into the lobby, "I saw you drive up. Hey, Janet, Harry. I was about to head over to your place."

"Why? Is it Summer? What's happened?" Janet asked urgently, immediately fearing the worst.

"Yeah, but don't panic. As far as I know Summer's okay. One of the deputies found her and Liam Taylor at the bottom of the hill just short of the main road. He transported them both to the hospital. Nothing serious though. I guess Summer fainted."

"Keith, we have to get over there."

"I've gotta stay here," Cain said quickly, "but I'll have one of my boys escort you in case you run into any problems. It's a mess out there."

"Thanks, Cain. I appreciate it," Keith said gratefully, trying to control the anxiety in his voice.

His wife and son needed to see him strong, but Keith was worried sick. He'd fallen in love with his baby girl the moment he'd laid eyes on her. He'd felt as if the tiny infant had cloaked him in a beam of golden sunlight, and with tears in his eyes, he had asked his beautiful wife if they could name her Summer.

"She'll be fine," Janet murmured, looping her arm through his elbow and breaking into his thoughts.

He couldn't fool his wife. Not for a second.

"Yeah, course she will, she is," Keith muttered, trying to calm his racing heart.

"She's tougher than all of us," Harry piped up. "She probably just, I dunno, tripped or something."

Harry had tried, but the tremble in his voice had been obvious, and shoving his hands into the pockets of his jacket he curled his fingers into white-knuckled fists.

* * *

When Summer passed out, Liam hastily popped both their boots from their bindings, pulled off his backpack, then sitting on the snow covered road, he'd brought her into his arms. She'd been vaguely conscious, and when he'd seen the large Hummer driving slowly towards them, if he hadn't already been on the ground, he would have dropped to his knees in a prayer of relief and gratitude. It had been a deputy sheriff out on patrol.

Scooping her up, Liam had carried her to the warmth and safety of the large SUV, placed her in the back seat, and held her as the deputy collected their skis.

"I'm Deputy Landon, I'll get you over to the hospital," the officer had declared, climbing behind the wheel. "You wanna tell me what you're doin' out here at daybreak?"

"My name's Liam Taylor. There's been an avalanche."

"Good to meet you Mr. Taylor...uh...you say there's been an avalanche? You sure? Where?"

"It started above my home on the knoll. I have no idea if it's a small slip or a major event. We were tryin' to get back to Summer's home when she collapsed."

"Dang. I need to radio that in. Is that Summer Brown? Keith Brown's daughter?"

"I don't know her father's name. Sorry."

"Yeah, I reckon it is. The Brown's are well-known around here. Mr. Brown's a good friend of the sheriff's."

As the deputy contacted the station, Summer had stirred in his arms.

"Are you okay, hon?"

"I think so. I just got all dizzy."

"You're totally worn out and hit the wall. I was gettin' there too. I'm surprised you didn't pass out sooner."

"I don't feel amazing."

"Trust me, you are."

"We're here, Mr. Taylor. Do you want me to take your skis to the station? You can pick them up there."

"That'd be great, thanks."

"What about your backpack?"

"I'll keep that with me."

"Okay. I'll carry it in for you."

Liam had packed a pair of shoes and a rolled up sweat suit, and after Summer had been settled into an emergency cubicle, he removed his boots and put on his trainers. Sitting at her bedside, he held her hand as they waited for the doctor.

"We made it," she murmured. "I can't believe it, but we did."

"Yep, we made it," he replied softly, "thanks to you."

"Oh, my gosh, mom," Summer suddenly muttered, her eyes widening as she looked past him.

Turning around, Liam saw three worried faces, obviously belonging to her parents and her brother.

"Sweetheart. Are you okay?" her mother asked as they moved next to the bed.

"Fine, I think, but how did you know I was here?"

"Hey, I'm Liam Taylor," Liam said quickly, rising to his feet. "Good to meet you all, but I'm sorry it's under these circumstances."

"Thanks for takin' care of my girl here," Keith said gratefully, immediately liking the handsome celebrity. "I'm Keith, this is Janet, and that's Harry."

"I think it's Summer who took care of me," Liam declared. "I'd still be in the house if it wasn't for her."

"Yeah, she does things like that," Harry remarked, staring at his sister.

"But who told you where I was, and how did you guys get here so fast?" Summer asked.

"The minute I got your email we high-tailed it over to the sheriff's office," her father replied, "and one of the deputies escorted us here, but sweetie, are you okay? What happened?"

"I got dizzy, then my legs gave out. I don't know why."

"The doctor should be here any minute," Liam said. "I'm gonna see if I can find some coffee and give you guys some time to catch up. Anyone else here want some?"

"Yeah, thanks," Harry piped up.

"Harry, go with Mr. Taylor and bring back coffee for me and tea for your mother," Keith said. "Make sure it's hot."

"Sure," Harry replied, then staring down at Summer, he added, "I'm glad you're okay, like, really glad."

"Thanks, Harry."

Liam saw Janet look away to wipe a tear from her cheek. Summer belonged to a close-knit family. It was heartwarming, and shooting her a quick wink, he left with Harry.

"Sure is quiet here," Liam said softly as they entered the gleaming corridor. "I guess it's still pretty early."

"Yeah, everyone's hunkered down from the storm, but, uh, it's cool to meet you," Harry said, grinning at him. "I'm a musician like Summer. I think it's great what you do."

"Thanks, Harry. What do you play?"

"Piano," Harry said simply. "Dad said Summer had one of her visions about the avalanche. Is that why you left your house on skis? Damn, that's gnarly."

"I didn't believe her at first, then I realized I had no choice. I mean, I couldn't afford not too. Turns out she was right, but you probably know what I'm talkin' about."

"Oh, yeah," Harry replied, rolling his eyes. "First time she did that with me was the mornin' I was supposed to try out for Little League. She came bustin' into my room and sat on top of me. She said I wasn't allowed to leave the house. Dad was home, thank God. He managed to warn everyone. No-one knew it was Summer who had the dream. He was already known for that hocus-pocus stuff so he took the blame."

"Don't you mean the credit?"

"People get weird about stuff like that."

"So—what happened?"

"A semi-truck lost control and crashed through the fence at the park. It hit the bleachers and went careening through the grounds. A lotta people would've been hurt—probably killed— if it hadn't been for Summer."

"Summer's visions, and your dad's, are they well-known around Apple Valley? I only moved here recently, but I spent time here when I was a kid and I don't remember anything like that."

"Just my dad. He didn't want Summer bein' treated differently and he still doesn't. She tells him what she sees, and then he does whatever. They don't happen often. It's been a couple of years since the last one."

"That was wise of your dad."

"Yeah, he's cool."

They'd reached the cafeteria, and grateful it was open so early, Liam walked straight to the coffee machine. The three women behind the counter pointed and whispered, but accustomed to the attention he barely noticed.

"Let's sit down a minute," he suggested, removing the cardboard cup from under the dispenser. "The doctor will probably be with Summer by now, and your parents should handle that by themselves."

"Sounds good," Harry agreed, making himself hot chocolate. "They tried to hide it, but they were really freaked out. I was too."

"Of course you were," Liam remarked as they settled into a table. "Tell me, Harry, what's your goal in life? Summer said you're in college, but not much more than that."

"I'm into classical music, though I like what Summer writes. She'll probably make a million bucks while I'll still be starvin'. I like playin' for her though, I like it a lot."

"You play when she sings?"

"Yeah. She's not great on the keyboard, that's why I did the YouTube thing for her."

"Summer did a YouTube video?"

"More than one. She has a channel. It's called Summer Sings. You haven't seen it?"

"No, she didn't mention it."

"Oh, God, she'll kill me. Don't tell her I said anything, I just assumed she would have."

"I won't say a word, but back to you. Who's your favorite composer?"

"Eric Satie," Harry said with a faraway look in his eye. "He's like the soul of classical music. That's what I wanna write, classical stuff with soul. I kinda changed up one of Summer's songs, One-Way Street, and it worked out great."

"Huh. That's interesting. Do you see yourself as part of a band, or do you wanna be a composer?"

"If I could find people who think like me it'd be fun to have a small orchestra. Classical music is where it's at for me, but like I said, I wanna do something with a bluesy feel that's current. It's hard to explain."

"You explained it just fine, and I think it's genius."

"Really?"

"The concept is great. If you can hear it in your head when you—"

"I totally hear it," Harry said eagerly, interrupting him. "I hear it all the time. I play in a rock band at college, but I do my classical stuff in hotels. It helps pay the bills, and I get ideas all the time. Music is what I wanna do. It's all I think about."

"It's a tough business."

"I know, but I still wanna give it a go. When I'm watchin' movies, I think how bad the score sucks and how I could've done so much better."

"Maybe that's your callin'. Don't worry, you're young. You'll find your niche."

"Thanks for sayin' that, Liam. I'm like Summer. I know in my heart music is what I'm supposed to be doin'."

"It's time we headed back with your dad's coffee and your mom's tea."

"Yeah, and I wanna find out what the doctor had to say."

As Harry returned to the machine and filled the cups, Liam moved up to the counter to pay. One of the women was brave enough to ask for his autograph, and he happily scribbled it on a piece of paper.

"Is that weird?" Harry asked as they left.

"No, and I'm always flattered. I came from nowheresville. Like you would say, it's cool."

"Can I ask you somethin'?"

"Sure."

"You and my sister, are you, like, together?"

"Are we together?" Liam murmured. "Yeah, I guess we are."

CHAPTER ELEVEN

When Liam and Harry returned, they found Janet and Keith looking much happier than when they'd left, and though Summer still appeared tired and pale, she was brighter.

"Liam, I'm glad you're back," Keith said warmly as Harry handed off the drinks.

"I take it the doctor was here," Liam remarked. "What did he say?"

"It's nothing serious," Janet replied, relief in her voice. "Summer's suffering from exhaustion. He said her immune system will be compromised so we need to be careful about colds and the flu and suchlike."

"I'm not surprised," Liam said solemnly. "When I found her trapped in her car off the side of the road she was a block of ice. It was hell gettin' her outta there in the blizzard, then we had to ski outta my place before dawn. The poor girl has been through the mill."

"I am here, you know," Summer quipped.

"Sorry honey," her father said with a grin. "The best news is, you can come home and we'll be together for Christmas, but you have to stay in bed and get plenty of rest."

"I'm not having Christmas dinner in bed. I'll be at the table. I'm not dying, I'm just tired."

"I think she's fine," Harry said with a chuckle.

"Liam, we were talkin'," Janet began tentatively. "You're very welcome to stay with us."

"That's very kind of you, but I couldn't impose."

"You were comin' to dinner anyway, and we'd like to have you, we really would," Keith said earnestly. "It's the least we can do. I'll feel bad thinkin' about you in a hotel over Christmas when we have the room."

"Please, you've gotta," Harry said earnestly. "I wanna play one of my compositions for you. I'd really love to hear what you think."

"Now, Harry, don't pester the man," Janet scolded. "We're not inviting him to put him to work. It's the holidays."

"Actually, Janet, it's not a problem. I'm interested in Harry's music. I was going to ask him to play for me at some point anyway."

"No shit?"

"Harry!" his father said sharply.

"Sorry. I wasn't expectin' that. Thanks, Mr. Taylor. I could really use your advice."

"Please say yes?"

Summer had spoken softly, but her ardent plea caught everyone's attention.

"You can't say no to that," Keith said with a chuckle. "That's how she got her first bicycle, and a whole lotta other stuff through the years."

"I can imagine," Liam replied with a wide grin, "and it looks like it's gonna work on me too. Thank you. I'd be delighted to stay, but it will probably be just for tonight. I'd like to fly back to my family in Nashville at some point tomorrow if I can. I was on my way to the airfield yesterday when I found Summer in the ditch. How soon will she be able to leave here?"

"Again...I'm here!" she exclaimed.

"Just about any time now," Janet replied, "and we should—" but before she could finish, she was cut off by the sound of a piano.

"My phone!" Harry declared excitedly, pulling it from his pocket. "We've got cell service back."

"Turn it off," Keith said sharply. "No phones are allowed in here."

"But dad, we have cell service!"

"Yeah, I heard you the first time."

"I'm goin' outside. I need to get my messages."

"I should check mine too," Liam remarked, picking up his backpack and unzipping one of the side compartments. "There has to be somewhere phones are allowed here."

"Maybe the stairwell," Keith suggested, "but accordin' to the nurse we'll only be here a few minutes."

"Not to worry, I won't be long," Liam assured him. "Summer, I'll see you shortly."

Though he didn't want to interrupt Frank or Wally's Christmas, Liam wanted to fly to Nashville as soon as possible. Not only did he want to be with his sister and parents, he needed some distance from Summer. He'd been drawn to her from the moment they'd met, but their white hot chemistry had taken him by surprise.

* * *

Growing impatient, Summer's mother left to find out what was keeping the nurse, and the moment she left, Keith settled in the chair next to Summer's bed, fixing her with a steady gaze.

"Okay, kitten, why were you headin' home in the middle of the mornin' yesterday? Was it because the storm was comin'?"

"Not exactly," she said with a heavy sigh.

"It's just you and me now. Tell me what's goin' on?"

"It's embarrassing," she murmured, dropping her eyes.

"You'll feel a whole lot better if you get it off your chest, and I'm sure it's not as bad as you think."

"I never did tell Liam why I knocked on his door."

"Did you chicken out?"

"Yeah. Totally. When I met him, I couldn't do it."

"What'd you tell him?"

"That I was looking for a job as a PA."

"Hey, it's okay, you're only human."

"I never expected him to hire me, but he did, so I started singing around the house so he could hear my voice, but that didn't work. Are you mad?"

"Of course not. I just feel bad that you were afraid to tell me."

"I felt stupid. I still feel stupid."

"Hey, you may be many things, kitten, but stupid isn't one of them. How does this relate to you leavin' early?"

"He heard me talking on the phone with Sandy, and he found out I'd lied to him. We had it out, and, uh..."

"You left."

"Yeah. I left, but there's more."

"I'm listenin'."

"He fired me."

"He what? Because of that?"

"No, no! Not because of that. He fired me because he said he wanted to go out with me, and he doesn't date people who work for him."

"Ah, well that's good, isn't it?"

"Dad, I'm crazy about him," she said in a hushed whisper, leaning forward and staring at him. "I mean, like, really. That's what I meant in my email. I don't care that he's Liam Taylor with a big house and tons of money. It's great and everything, but it's him I care about, not all that other stuff. Dad, he's...he's...oh, my gosh, he's just the best, and it wouldn't matter if he was a vet, or a trucker, or a rancher, it wouldn't matter one bit, and you know what?"

"I'm almost afraid to ask."

"I knew it when he opened the door that first day. I think that's why I was too scared to ask him if he'd hear me sing. I took one look at him and I got this really weird feeling in my stomach."

"It can happen like that," he murmured knowingly. "Does he feel the same?"

"I think so, I mean, yeah. It seems like he does."

"He'd better treat you right," Keith said, suddenly needing to hug her. "If he doesn't he'll have a big problem on his hands. Damn. I guess my little girl's all grown up. I can't believe it."

"I'll always be your little girl. That's never going to change."

"I know baby," he said softly, trying to fight the sudden surge of emotion rippling through his heart and heating up his throat. "I know."

* * *

Liam hadn't meant to listen.

When he was about to walk through the curtain and heard Keith having a father-daughter talk, he'd turned to leave, but something made him stop. He knew it was wrong to eavesdrop, but at that moment he didn't care.

Liam Taylor was responsible for selling millions of records and managed some of the biggest names in the country and western music scene. He wielded power and influence, and was extremely wealthy, but as his fame had exploded, he had found himself doubting the sincerity of others, especially the women who graced his bed.

The uncertainty was like an unseen shadow, and as he listened to Summer's heartfelt confession, Liam hadn't just felt a sudden sense of freedom and a huge wave of relief, he'd felt his guard dropping away.

Moving silently from the curtain and out into the corridor, he leaned against the wall and took several deep breaths. His heart had never felt so full. He wanted to race back to Summer's bed and hug her and kiss her and tell her how amazing she was.

Glancing up and down the hallway, he thought how bizarre it was that he was feeling such joy while completely alone and in such an incongruous place, but he knew it was a moment he'd never forget. Leaning against the wall and running his fingers through his hair, he decided the saying, God works in mysterious ways, was never more appropriate. He'd only returned to Summer's bedside because he'd discovered he was missing a glove. He'd assumed he'd dropped it next to her bed.

"Liam?"

Straightening up, he saw Janet walking swiftly towards him.

"Yeah, I'm missin' a glove," he blurted out, then realized how bizarre it had sounded. "I stuffed them into my pockets but now I've only got one."

"I think I saw it. We're done here. We can get Summer home."

"That's great."

Trying to gather his wits, he followed her in and found Summer climbing into a wheelchair. Hospital policy decreed the patient be wheeled outside. She looked as happy and relieved as he felt. The unburdening of her soul had done wonders.

"Hi there," she said smiling up at him. "Did you have a ton of messages?"

"So many I didn't listen to any of them, and I've lost a glove."

"Oh, I have it. Dad found it on the floor. Losing a glove is so annoying."

"It can be," he nodded, "but not this time."

"How so?"

"I'll tell you later."

CHAPTER TWELVE

Liam showered and changed the moment he returned with Summer and her family to their house. Grateful he'd thought to pack a change of clothes, he ambled down to the kitchen and joined everyone at the table for breakfast, but still exhausted, both he and Summer returned to their respective rooms for some much needed sleep.

Liam was the first to surface in the early afternoon. Janet and Keith were expecting guests for Christmas dinner and the dining room table had been set for ten. Preparations were in full swing, and he was delighted to pitch in and help.

"I hope it won't be too terrible for you," Janet said with a worried frown. "I'm sure you'll be deluged with questions."

"I'm used to questions," he replied with a grin. "It's fine, really. I'm very happy to be here."

And he was.

Sitting on the road holding Summer semi-conscious in his arms, he'd had moments of grave fear. Exhausted from the perilous journey, he wasn't sure how far he'd be able to carry her, nor the distance the avalanche might travel. Now Summer was safe, and he had been warmly welcomed into her home.

She reappeared when the guests began arriving. The sparkle had returned to her eyes, and dressed in black pants and a red Christmas sweater with Rudolph emblazoned on the front, he longed to wrap her into his arms and give her an endless Christmas kiss. Sitting next to her at the dinner table, he couldn't remember feeling so close to a woman. The intimacy was unfamiliar to him, but it was one he joyfully embraced. To his surprise, the guests' fascination of him and his life lasted only a few minutes before the conversation turned to the horrific storm and avalanche.

"It's a miracle Summer and Liam made it out," her mother remarked solemnly. "I don't know how they managed to ski all the way down that hill to the main road in the dark. It must have been such a frightening ordeal."

"We had an angel on our shoulder," Liam said gratefully, "and you're right. The entire night was filled with miracles. I can't tell you how relieved I felt when that deputy showed up out of nowhere."

Summer's knee unexpectedly pressed against his, then a moment later her hand tickled his inner thigh. He glanced around the table. Deep in conversation, no-one paid them any attention.

Suddenly her fingers crawled upwards and pressed against his cock.

Energy surged through his loins.

He tried to think of a discreet way to make her stop.

Nothing came to mind.

His member stiffened.

If they'd been in a restaurant, he would have marched her out to the parking lot and soundly spanked her in the back of his car. Seated around a dining room table with her family and friends he was helpless.

The meal had begun with soup. When everyone finished, Janet and Keith collected the empty bowls and disappeared into the kitchen. Deciding to spill his drink over his lap, Liam reached for his water glass, but Keith returned carrying the impressive turkey, and a moment later Janet arrived with the side dishes.

The opportunity had passed.

"Thank you for comin' today," Keith announced, holding up a dangerous-looking knife. "It's wonderful to be surrounded by old friends, and welcome a new one," he added, smiling across at Liam. "Every year my beautiful wife worries that the bird won't be cooked properly. Of course it's always perfect, and I'm sure this year will be no exception, but before I start slicin' I'm gonna share some news. Janet, will you stand next to me, hon?"

"What's this all about?" she asked, rising from her chair.

"You'll find out in a minute," he murmured, putting his arm around her waist. "As you all know I've spent the last three years goin' back and forth to Iraq, Afghanistan and Germany. It's been tough, but I'm happy to announce my globetrottin' is over. I'm gonna be workin' at the base thirty minutes from Apple Valley. Honey, your hubby is home."

Janet stared at him, her eyes wide, but only for a second before she threw her arms around his neck and buried her face in his shoulder. The entire table broke into loud chatter, raising their glasses and offering their congratulations.

Liam seized the chance.

He was about to grab Summer's wrist and jerk it from his turgid member when she jumped from her chair and hurried around the table to hug her father. Relieved she was no longer torturing him, Liam raised his champagne glass in a toast, but when she sat back down, she immediately dropped her hand back to his crotch. Lowering his head, he whispered in her ear.

"If your hand isn't on the table in three-seconds, you won't sit for a week."

A hot pink flush flamed across her face, and she quickly pulled her hand away, but as the dinner continued, she fell oddly quiet.

"What's on your mind?" Liam asked as the meal began to wind down.

"I probably shouldn't say this," she murmured, "but I'm upset that you're leaving. It doesn't seem right."

"I wish there were two of me, but I'll be back after New Years."

"New Years!" she said with a heavy sigh. "You're probably going to some big shindig."

"You could say that. Every year my company throws a party, and bein' the boss I've gotta be there, but I'll be back real quick. I know I'll miss you, and God only knows how many tons of snow are sittin' on top of my house." Then pausing thoughtfully, he added, "You know, Summer, if you're not too busy, maybe you could help me."

"I did have a job, but I just got fired, so I have plenty of time on my hands. Can you believe someone would fire me on Christmas Eve? Talk about a Scrooge!"

"Who would do a thing like that?" he said with a chuckle. "I can only assume you must've been a very bad girl."

"I plead the fifth."

"Probably smart," he retorted with a devilish grin. "How would you feel about me hirin' you back for a couple of weeks?"

"Maybe, if I get a raise."

"Oh, yeah? How much of a raise?"

"Double, no, triple," she said with a giggle. "Of course I'll help you, but I don't want to be paid. That would be weird. Just tell me what to do and I'll do it."

The thought of working with him on his house had brightened her up, but just a few minutes later, out of the blue, she let out a long yawn and rested her head on his shoulder.

"Are you fadin', sugar?"

"I am," she said wearily. "My bones feel heavy."

"Summer?" her mother called from across the table. "What's wrong, honey?"

"I just got tired all of a sudden."

"You need to get back to bed," Keith declared. "Doctor's orders, re-member? Lots of rest."

"I hate to leave, but I think you're right. Thanks for a great meal, mom. It was one of the best ever."

"It was one of the best ever because you were here in one piece. Now go and get some rest."

"I'll see you up the stairs," Liam offered, and rising from his chair, he walked her from the room.

* * *

After a long hug and lingering kiss, Summer stretched out on her bed. Sitting next to her, Liam suddenly found himself in conflict. He wanted to get back to Nashville and be with his family, but he was torn. He and Summer had connected, and her comment was swimming around his head.

I'm upset that you're leaving. It doesn't seem right.

He was feeling the same way.

Could he take her with him?

Not really, she was still recovering.

"Liam?"

"Yep?"

"You look worried."

"I gotta tell you, sugar, I don't wanna take off. Like you said, it doesn't feel right."

"Do you have to go?"

"I'd disappoint my family, and I do want to see them. Then there's the party. I have people doin' the organizin', but there are always last minute hitches only I can deal with."

"Then, you have to take off. It's a bummer though."

"What's that music?"

"That will be Harry. You should hear him. He's so good. I mean, really good."

"And you're lookin' like you're about to pass out."

"I think I am."

"Get some sleep, and you'd better believe I'm gonna be spankin' your butt as soon as you're better. Puttin' your hand under the table and tormentin' me like that. Shame on you."

"Uh-huh," she said with a wink. "It was fun though."

"For you, maybe. You will be spanked, and soundly, you bad girl. Now get some rest."

He kissed her softly, then ambling from the room and closing the door behind him, he headed down the stairs. Harry's music became clearer, and reaching the living room, he stopped outside the door.

Harry was something special.

Very special.

The composition was complex, the chord changes unpredictable, yet the melody carried a compelling flow.

There was no question in Liam's mind.

He wanted to help Harry any way he could.

Closing his eyes and leaning against the wall, Liam lost himself in the mellifluous music, and when the piece came to an end he was sorry it was over. Taking a breath, he walked into the living room.

"Harry, I'm impressed. Quite honestly I've never heard anything like it. Sort of, Chopin meets Coldplay."

"You really liked it?"

"I did."

"Cool. Thanks, Liam. Wow."

But the guests were starting to leave. Rising from his seat at the piano, Harry joined Keith and Janet to escort them to the front door.

Sitting down, Liam tinkled on the keys, then idly looked through the music on top of the piano.

A One-Way Street.

The song Harry had mentioned.

Picking it up, he caught his breath.

Underneath the title, were the words, A Song For Liam.

He started to read the lyrics, but Janet, Keith and Harry reappeared and he quickly dropped the sheet of paper.

"Hey, Liam," Keith said, strolling up to him, "would you like to check on your house? The snowplows will have cleared that road by now."

"That would be great, thanks, Keith," Liam said gratefully. "I'm anxious to see it, assuming we can get there."

"Can I come?" Harry asked hopefully.

"I'd rather you stay and help your mother clear up. Let me see if I can find a jacket for you, Liam."

As Keith marched from the room Liam started to follow, but abruptly turned back to Harry.

"I'm gonna be in Nashville until after New Year's and I've asked Summer to supervise gettin' my home back in order. Maybe you can help her out."

"Sure. Yeah. I'd be happy to," Harry said eagerly.

"Great. I'd better catch up to your dad. I'll see you later."

But it wasn't his house that was in the forefront of his mind.

A Song For Liam.

He was sure it had been the original title.

A part of him wanted to read the lyrics, but there was that old adage about letting sleeping dogs lie.

CHAPTER THIRTEEN

The snowplows had done their job, and as Keith drove through the residential community, Liam eyed the high piles of snow lining the road.

"Have you ever seen it like this before?" Liam asked as Keith turned the corner and started through town.

"Never, and I've been livin' here almost thirty years," he replied, then pausing, he added, "It's good to see Summer so happy."

"She's a terrific girl."

"I sure think so, although that comes with my job title," Keith said with a grin, "but I'm mighty proud of her. She could've left home a while ago, but with Harry off at school and me away so much, she wanted to stay with her mother. She's like that. Real thoughtful. Now I'm home for good she can finally spread her wings."

Keith's comment was subtle and obvious at the same time, but Liam's mind abruptly switched gears.

"Keith, can I talk to you about Harry for a minute?"

"Sure. I'm real proud of him too. He's a talented kid."

"He is, but he has more than just talent. His music is unique. If he sticks with it he'll go places."

"Really? Damn. I wasn't expecting that."

"Harry's music has the X factor. What I heard is still rattlin' around in my head. If it's all right with you I'd like to put him in touch with one of my producers. I think he might be able give Harry a leg up."

"Damn, Liam, that would be great. Harry would be thrilled. Everyone raves about Summer's voice and her songs, but they don't relate to him the same way. He adores her, but he's been livin' in her shadow and that's been hard on him."

"I have a feeling he won't be in Summer's shadow much longer," Liam remarked as they approached the road that led up the hill to his house. "Will you look at that! Whatta relief. I thought this whole area would be closed off."

"Yeah, I did too," Keith murmured, turning up the slope and driving forward, "but it doesn't look like the slide came anywhere near here. It must have gone through the forest."

"A couple more turns and you'll see where Summer went into the ditch."

"I still can't believe you found her."

"You and me both. It's just around this bend. Holy smokes!" Liam exclaimed as Keith slowed. "There's nothin' but piles of snow. Man! It gives me the willies just lookin' at it."

"Me too," Keith said gravely, continuing up the hill.

"My house will be around this next sweepin' turn," Liam said, his heart starting to pump. "You'll see the tall gates on your left. There...whoa! I don't believe it! How is that even possible?"

"Now that's a sight. You got your phone? Take a picture, take a bunch of pictures."

"I'm already pullin' it out." Bizarrely-shaped, huge chunks of snow littered the grounds, and half of the roof resembled a ski-lift. "Why didn't the avalanche fall straight down the mountain and bury this place?"

"If you look over there," Keith said, pointing to a nearby forest, "that seems to have taken the brunt of it. Thank the Lord there are no homes in that area. You should call in the experts, though they'll probably show up when word gets out. An avalanche here is pretty wild."

"Summer said there have been a couple in the past."

"The two she's talkin' about were on a different peak. This is a freak thing."

"Maybe there's a way to mitigate any further threat. I'm gonna have Summer track down the folks who know about this stuff. I wonder if it's safe to climb over the fence and try to get to my house. I guess I should've brought my skis."

"I'd suggest you call Cain and ask for his help. The county boys will be comin' out anyway, but Cain will be able to get them here quicker."

"I've gotta say, I'm relieved. It's bad, but not as bad as I thought it'd be. At least the studio is in the basement, but on the other side," he said solemnly, "it looks like the roof might've caved. That's where my bedroom is, or rather was."

"You saved Summer from her car, she saved you from the avalanche, then you both managed to get out. That's quite a story for your first Christmas together."

Keith's remark hit home.

Your first Christmas together.

It suggested there would be more.

The thought made his heart swell.

"Have you seen enough?" Keith asked.

"Yeah, sure," Liam replied. "Now I need to call my pilot. Hopefully we'll be able to take off soon."

"I heard you have your own plane," Keith said, turning the car around and heading back down. "I've done some flyin' myself. Can I ask what it is?"

"A Gulfstream G550."

"Nice. I'm surprised our little airport can handle that."

"A few of the farmers around here got together and extended the runway a couple of years back."

"Damn. You're right. Slipped my mind."

"I couldn't have bought property here without an airfield that could handle my plane," Liam continued, placing the call. "I've got so much goin' on I need—excuse me. Hey, Frank. Merry Christmas. What's the word? Any chance we can take off tomorrow?"

Glancing at Keith as he continued the conversation, Liam understood the smile crossing the man's lips. He was home for good, his daughter had survived a brush with death, and a door had opened for his son.

"Hey, Keith, when do you think the county will be out?" Liam asked as he ended his call.

"Probably the day after tomorrow. Knowing them, they'll need twenty-four hours to recover from the holiday."

"Dammit, I should be here."

"Do you really have to leave?"

"Yeah, but I've learned to accept there's only one of me and I can't be everywhere. I'll leave the keys with Summer."

"She'll be able to start organizin' things for you once you know what's what, but I'm not sure she's up to dealin' with the boys from the county, and the city fellas will be out as well. I'm happy to meet them for you."

"Keith, that's very generous of you, but won't you be busy? You've been gone for months."

"Liam, you rescued my daughter from a car in a blizzard, and you're giving my son an important helpin' hand. It's the least I can do, besides, I'll know these guys. I might be able to cut through some red tape for you."

"That would be great, Keith, thank you. I appreciate it very much."

"When do you think you'll be back?"

"Hard to say, but hopefully the first week of January."

"I can't believe New Year's is around the corner," Keith muttered. "I'm still not sure what I'm gonna do about that. I've been tryin' to figure out where to send Harry and Summer."

"You need to send them somewhere?"

"I don't need to, it's just...well...the thing is, in February Janet and I will celebrate our twenty-fifth weddin' anniversary, and I haven't had her to myself on New Year's Eve since Summer was born. That's twenty-two years. I'm hopin' to finally make that happen."

"Why don't you go out of town?"

"I thought about that, but I'd rather take her to a nice meal and come home. Then we can lie around in the mornin'...maybe I'll even make her breakfast in bed. I just want the house to ourselves for a bit."

"I'm sure you'll figure it out. You seem like a resourceful man."

"Yep, that's me," Keith said with a chuckle. "Mr. Resourceful."

"How have you managed to stay together so long?" Liam asked as Keith rolled into his driveway.

"Ha, that's easy. I always make sure Janet knows I love her to bits, and she's the only woman I ever wanted, but more importantly we've learned how to forgive and forget. The forgettin' part, that's the key."

"You're an inspiration," Liam said softly. "There's a song in there somewhere. I'm gonna give those lines to one of my writers. If anything comes of it you'll be gettin' a royalty."

"Maybe I'll have my fifteen minutes of fame along with my kids. I wouldn't say no to that."

Climbing from the car and walking into the kitchen, they were met with the tempting aroma of fresh coffee.

"You're back!" Janet declared, kissing Keith on the cheek.

"How was your house? Was there a crazy amount of snow?" Harry asked excitedly. "Could you even get up that road?"

"It wasn't as bad as I thought it would be," Liam replied, removing his coat and sitting at the kitchen table, "but it's a bizarre scene. I'll show you the pictures. Man, I'm suddenly beat."

"After everything you've been through the last twenty-four hours, I'm not surprised," Janet remarked, placing a steaming mug of coffee in front of him.

"Yeah. I guess so. I think I'll go upstairs and take a load off, but first I'd like a quick chat with you Harry, if you have a minute."

"Sure."

"Janet, Keith, will you join us?"

"Of course," Keith replied as Janet wiped her hands and sat down.

"This might sound strange," Liam began, "but when I hear a song, or even just a melody, it speaks to me or it doesn't, and Harry, your music didn't speak to me. It shouted."

"Wow. Thanks, Liam."

"I'd like to put you in touch with a producer I work with. He'll know what to do with you, how to channel what you have into something commercial—that's if you're interested."

"Yeah, of course I'm interested. Wow. This is so cool!"

"His name is Scott Bridges. If you give me your email address I'll put you in touch with each other. Do you know how to upload an audio sample?"

"Sure, I do it all the time, and I've got stuff on YouTube as well."

"Great. Send him the link, and upload four pieces. Make them different. Show him a range."

"Oh, man, this is, wow, this is fantastic. I don't know what to say. Thank you, thank you so much."

"You're welcome. I'll be followin' what you guys do together very closely. Your music isn't in my ballpark, but Scott will know what to do with it."

"Liam, how can we ever thank you?" Janet asked earnestly. "This is so unexpected, and, well, my goodness. I don't know what else to say."

"It's what I do," Liam replied. "Findin' new talent is a rush. I love it. Now if you'll excuse me, I am seriously wiped out."

"We're mighty grateful," Keith added, "and you do look kinda beat. Go up and get some rest."

"Yep, I'm gonna do exactly that," Liam said, stretching as he rose to his feet.

Suddenly jumping from the table, Harry awkwardly extended his hand, then unable to control his excitement and gratitude, he threw his arms around Liam and hugged him.

"You don't know what this means to me. Thank you! Thank you so much."

"Hey, Harry," Liam replied, "I'm just glad I found you before anyone else."

* * *

Leaving the kitchen and climbing the stairs, though his muscles ached and his head was beginning to thump, Liam stopped at Summer's door and slowly cracked it open. Under the covers and sound asleep, she looked like an angel. Wishing he could crawl between the sheets and snuggle next to her, he let out a weary sigh and moved on to his room.

He'd slipped his Macbook into his knapsack. Pulling it out, he kicked off his shoes and laid on the bed. Sinking into the comfortable mattress, he wanted to close his eyes and drift away, but he knew there'd be a ton of emails waiting for him. Opening the computer, he clicked into his mailbox.

Skimming through the many messages and finding nothing urgent, he sent a quick note to his sister with a brief update, and told her he'd be arriving home late afternoon the following day. Closing the laptop, he placed it on the bedside table and settled in for his nap. At some point he felt a chill and slipped under the covers, vaguely thinking it was probably time to go back downstairs.

But that didn't happen.

When he finally woke up it was morning.

He'd slept for over fifteen hours.

CHAPTER FOURTEEN

Liam stared at his wrist. His watch. Where was it?

Still in a groggy daze, he rolled over and found it sitting on his laptop. He had no memory of taking it off, then realized he'd slept in his clothes. Rubbing his hand over his face, he tried to remember where he'd put his phone, then suddenly felt it in his pocket. Letting out a loud yawn and pulling it out, he squinted and stared at the screen. 10:02 a.m. Sitting up, he checked his messages. He had three texts from Frank.

Wheels up noon. Please confirm.

Liam? We're set. Is that good?

Okay, now I'm starting to worry. Get back to me.

They'd been sent about thirty minutes apart. He immediately tapped in his response.

Overslept. Confirmed.

Leaving the phone next to his watch, he quickly rose from the bed, and still in disbelief he'd slept so deeply for so long, he headed into the bathroom.

* * *

Summer hadn't stirred since she'd crawled into bed after Christmas dinner. Slowly waking up, her first thought was Liam. Though she didn't know when he'd be leaving, she knew it would be soon.

"No," she murmured under her breath. "I don't want you to go."

Sitting up and stretching her arms above her head, she rubbed her face and looked at her bedside clock. 10:35 a.m. Amazed she'd been out of it for so long, she slipped from the bed and padded off to take a shower. Longing to see Liam, she made it a quick one, then throwing on jeans and a sweater, she hurried down the stairs. Reaching the hall she could hear voices coming from the kitchen, and with the smell of bacon wafting through the air, she quickened her pace. Walking in the kitchen, she found her father and brother sitting at the table with Liam, and her mother standing at the stove.

"You're finally up," her mother declared. "How are you feeling? Are you hungry? I'm making Liam some breakfast."

"I feel fine, and yes, please, I'm starving."

"Good morning," Liam said with a warm smile. "You slept a long time."

"No kidding. What have I missed?" she asked as she sat down. "How's your house?"

Pulling out his phone, Liam began showing her the photographs he'd taken the previous day. When she saw the back of the roof under a ton of snow, she caught her breath.

"Oh, my gosh. That's what I saw in my vision," she declared. "That's where I was standing, on the roof, watching snow hurtling towards me."

"That's truly amazing," Liam said solemnly, staring at her. "Thank God you did."

"Thank God you believed me and didn't think I was crazy."

"Only for a minute or two," he said with a wink, trying to lighten things up. "Besides, I felt like a good ski."

"Hah, that's funny," Harry said with a chuckle.

"The good news is," Liam continued, "the house was hit either by a separate small slide, or just the edge of the avalanche. The road wasn't affected, and you can see where it impacted the forest a short ways off. I'm feeling very fortunate."

"Thank goodness," Janet said, as she placed a platter of scrambled eggs, fried tomatoes and bacon on the table. "Summer, would you like tea or coffee?"

"Tea, thanks. Um, Liam, are you planning to take off today?"

"I am, and I have to leave here shortly. We're lliftin' off at noon. I'll leave you the keys to my house."

"We'll go over there together, Summer," Keith interjected. "I'm gonna meet the guys from the county and the city. Hopefully I can get them there at the same time."

"Hey, dad, can I come?" Harry asked eagerly. "I really wanna see it. I did a bunch of research on avalanches last night."

"Sure, you can come."

As they chatted about the bizarre event, Summer devoured her breakfast, and though she tried to remain upbeat she found it difficult.

"Janet, thank you," Liam said gratefully, laying his knife and fork across his empty plate. "That was delicious."

"You're very welcome."

"I'd better get upstairs and make sure I haven't forgotten anything."

"Do you need a razor?" Keith asked. "I have a ton of them."

"No, I have one with me. I threw a few things into that backpack, but I think I'll wait until I get home."

"I like you unshaven," Summer said staring at him. "It suits you. It makes you look—"

"Unkempt?"

"No," she said with giggle. "It makes you look...um...rugged. That's the word. It makes you look rugged."

"Really? Huh. Well this rugged guy needs to get himself together."

"Dad, if it's all right with you," Summer began, "I'd like to take Liam to the airport?"

"Are you sure you're feelin' okay? You're not too tired?"

"Good grief, I just slept for fifteen hours," she declared, then leaning forward, she stared at her father with wide eyes. "I promise I'll drive extra carefully."

"There it is," Keith grinned. "See that, Liam? And it works every time."

"Yeah, so I'm learnin'."

"Thanks, dad. Actually, I should get changed too," she exclaimed, and downing her last swallow of tea, she pushed back from the table and moved swiftly from the room.

"Why did she need to change?" Harry muttered, shaking his head. "Women! There's something wrong with them, except for you, mom. You're perfect."

"You got that right," Keith exclaimed. "Your mother is...what's that phrase? Perfection personified."

"And on that note, I will see you all shortly," Liam said, rising from his chair. "Thanks again for the breakfast, Janet. It hit the spot."

Striding from the kitchen, he trotted up the stairs, but as he turned down the hall, he found Summer leaning against her door.

"That took you long enough," she said softly, grabbing his arm and pulling him into her bedroom.

"What are you—?"

Before he could finish, she threw her arms around his neck, crushed his lips in a fervent kiss, and tried to drag him to the bed.

"No, Sugar, we can't," he protested, pulling back. "Not here."

"Sorry, you're right," she said with a heavy sigh. "I just can't stand that you're taking off already."

"I don't wanna leave you either," he muttered. "We've just had this amazing, crazy time together, and now I have to go. It doesn't feel right."

"No, it doesn't."

"I promise I'll get back the minute I can, and I'm dependin' on you to get my house squared away, but let's get outta here," he added abruptly. "Maybe we'll have enough time for some foolin' around at the airfield."

"Is there somewhere we can do that?"

"Yep."

"I'll be downstairs in five minutes."

"Me too."

* * *

A short time later, as Liam and Summer stood by the car ready to head to the airfield, Janet hugged him, Keith shook his hand, and Harry wished him a safe trip. As they climbed in and headed down the main road, Liam told Summer he'd offered Harry a helping hand.

"Your brother's music is unique. I think he can go places."

"I agree, not that I know the business like you do."

"Honestly, I wouldn't know where to start with him, but I'm puttin' him in touch with a producer who will. A guy who has a love of classical and the blues just like your brother."

"I wondered why he was in such a good mood. Thanks, Liam."

"Summer, please don't feel put out. I told you I need to keep my business and my personal life separate, and I still do. I just think Scott can help your brother. It's an introduction, that's it."

"Liam, it's fine, I promise. You may find this hard to believe, but I really am only interested in you, as in, you Liam, not you Liam Taylor, Country Music Guru."

"You don't have to worry, Summer," he said, lowering his voice. "I believe you, and one of these days I'll tell you why."

"That sounds mysterious."

"It's not, but enough about that. Don't miss the turn-off, it's just up ahead."

"I know exactly where it is, oh, wow, is that your jet?"

"Yep."

"Can I look inside?"

"You certainly can, In fact—I insist."

"Oh, my gosh, how great is this?" she exclaimed, rolling into the parking lot, "but there's so much snow here. Are you sure it's safe to take off?"

"It might be cold and gray, but there's no messy weather."

Climbing from the car and moving into the small terminal building, Liam spotted Frank and Wally engrossed in conversation.

"Is everything good?" Liam asked as he approached.

"Yeah, great," Frank replied, "but we have thirty-five minutes before we need to start things rolling."

"This is Summer Brown, Summer, this is Frank, my pilot, and Wally, the airfield manager. I'm gonna show Summer the jet."

"Okay. I'll be there in about half-an-hour."

"Nice to meet you," Summer said, but barely got the words out before Liam took her hand and led her to the jet.

Walking up to the waiting steps, Liam gestured for her to enter ahead of him.

"Wow, this is gorgeous," she exclaimed, stepping into the aircraft.

"Keep movin' forward into that next compartment," he said, tossing his backpack on one of the front seats.

Following her through to the second cabin, he pushed a button at the base of the partition. A panel slid closed, giving them complete privacy.

"Liam, this is fantastic."

"We need a proper goodbye," he muttered, grabbing her around the waist and jerking her against him, "and someone needs a spankin' for bein' a very bad girl at the dinner table yesterday."

"But—uh— that was just for fun."

"Fun for you!"

"It was fun for you as well. You can't pretend you didn't like it."

"Young lady, your gorgeous ass is gonna pay for that fun," he declared, hustling her to a couch. "I'm not leavin' without makin' sure your butt is good and red."

"Liam, I—"

But suddenly fisting her hair, he devoured her mouth in a fervid kiss.

"You what?" he breathed, pulling back.

"N-nothing," she stammered.

"I didn't think so."

Dropping his hands to unbutton her slacks and slide down the zipper, her thick wool pants fell around her legs.

"Black lace panties. Nice," he declared, grabbing her wrist and jerking her over his lap.

Hastily moving them to her thighs, he landed his hand smartly on the center of her naked backside.

"Ouch!"

"No yellin'. Frank might step on board."

"He won't come back here, will he?"

"Nope, not with the door closed."

Raising his hand, Liam went to work, delivering his discipline with rapid-fire slaps, continuing without pause until her bottom was hot and blushing red. She had squirmed and hissed through her teeth, but she hadn't yelped loudly or begged him to stop.

"There, that should do it," he declared. "Now take off your clothes and sit on my cock."

Watching her crawl from his lap, pull off her sweater and pop off her bra, he withdrew a condom from his pocket and quickly removed his trousers and underwear. Sliding the thin sheath over his rigid member, he held himself in place as she lowered herself down.

Gazing at her luscious breasts, a surge of energy rippled through his loins. Hastily moving his mouth to her nipples, he lightly nipped, then hungrily devoured them, moving from breast to breast as he grasped her waist. Holding her tightly, he controlled her movements, sometimes holding her still as he pumped, other times making her ride him.

But he knew they were running out of time.

"Get on the floor," he said gruffly. "Raise yourself up on your hands and knees."

Dropping on all fours, he hurriedly kneeled behind her, grasped her hips, and plunged back inside her.

"Remember, no noise," he reminded her as she let out a cry. "Rub your clit. I'm gonna fuck you hard until you come, but we've gotta be quick."

Beginning with strong thrusts, he accelerated until he was vigorously pumping, frequently landing hot smacks. As she began bleating his name, he could feel his cock nearing its bursting point.

"I'm almost there," she panted breathlessly. "Please don't stop."

"I'm not stoppin," he growled. "I'm sending you over the edge."

Pulling a cheek aside, he thrust his finger into her dark hole. In spite of his reminder to stay quiet she let out a loud squeal, then suddenly convulsed beneath him. As her body shuddered, he exploded, gritting his teeth and swallowing back his groans.

* * *

A moment later, lying breathlessly and resting against Liam's shoulder, Summer let out a heavy sigh and murmured his name.

"What is it, sugar?"

"I hate that you're going away," she murmured, "but this helped. It helped a lot."

"It helped me too, and as much as I hate to say it, we need to get dressed."

Slowly rising to their feet and pulling on their clothes, he gave her a moment to run her fingers through her hair, then opened the partition. Moving into the front cabin, they settled into the seats, and he explained the various controls in the armrests.

"Five minutes and it's wheels up," Frank declared, entering into the plane and calling down the cabin.

"You heard the man," Liam said softly. "Time's up."

"I should be used to goodbyes," she lamented, "but they never get any easier."

"I'll be back before you know it," he promised, "and hey, we've had an amazing Christmas? It was crazy—scary—wild—but look what came out of it."

"It was the best," she managed, swallowing back the lump in her throat.

"I'll see you soon, sweet girl."

"Oh, I love that—sweet girl."

"It's why I call you sugar, sugar."

* * *

A little while later, standing in the terminal watching the plane taxi away and launch into the air, Summer felt both elated and forlorn, but a new song began singing itself in her head.

CHAPTER FIFTEEN
Nashville

Swirling his cognac, Liam stared into the flames dancing sensuously in the large fireplace. Taking a sip, he let the spicy, velvety smooth liquor rest on this tongue, tasting orange, cloves and another flavor he couldn't define. Finally swallowing, the high end brandy warmed his body. Sinking into his favorite chair as he listened to the soft rain outside, though he was happy to be in his Nashville home, he missed Summer.

He'd spent the day and evening with his sister Marie, her husband, Eric, and their two kids, Elise, five, and Kevin, nine. His niece and nephew had barraged him with endless questions about the vavadanche, as Elise had called it, until they were hustled off to bed. He wished his parents were there for the holidays, but he had no regrets. Their Christmas present was a luxury cruise in the South Pacific. They'd enjoy warm summer breezes and soft sandy beaches. His mother didn't do well in the cold.

Once the children had been tucked safely in their bed, Liam was free to talk to Marie and Eric about Summer. His sister and her husband were his closest friends. Eric was an entertainment lawyer specializing in the music business. It had been Liam who had introduced them. As he relayed the events, Marie leaned forward with a bemused look on her face.

"My little brother has fallen hard," she'd remarked. "I'm glad. It's about time."

"I think you're right," he'd admitted, "and it's unfamiliar territory."

"I'm sure. You and your revolving door."

"Okay, Marie. You've made your point."

"So, what are you going to do now?"

"Now I'm gonna take myself home."

"You've shared enough?" she'd quipped.

"Yeah...that."

"Are you sure you don't want to stay over?"

"No. I need to go, but thanks."

Eric hadn't commented, but that hadn't surprised Liam. Returning home, he'd changed into a comfortable sweat suit, ambled into his den, and lit the fire. Now sipping his expensive, one hundred year old cognac, he needed to think. He was wrestling with a dilemma.

Summer had a youtube channel.

To watch it, or not to watch it?

A Song For Liam had been haunting him since he'd seen the innocent sheet of music on top of the piano.

He was torn, and not just about what the lyrics of the song might say.

If she was an average singer there'd be no problem, but if she was great...?

Swirling his glass, he took another drink, then glancing across at the grandfather clock against the wall next to the bookshelves, he saw it was almost 10:20 p.m. Marie would still be up. She had always been his voice of reason. His eyes traveled to the burled-walnut box sitting on the bottom shelf. Inside was a piece of jewelry he'd bought in the same dusty antique store where he'd found the clock.

He'd been recording in England, and renting a car he'd traveled into the countryside for a few days of uninterrupted exploration. The shop had been in a small village, and the moment he'd laid eyes on the ring it had captured his imagination. He knew it would one day grace the finger of the woman who would steal his heart.

The setting was gold, and boasted a large deep-red ruby surrounded by alternating tiny pearls and diamonds. The bespectacled storekeeper, who could have stepped out of a Charles Dickens novel, had told Liam the ring had come from the sale of a centuries-old manor house. Liam believed him. It reeked of age, and when he'd had it valued on his return home, the jeweler appraised it at four times what he'd paid. Intrigued, he had contacted a British antique jewelry sleuth. After several weeks he'd received the report.

The ring had revolved around a real-life Romeo and Julie story. Dating back to the 17th century, it had been commissioned by an Earl for his secret beloved, a young Countess named Victoria Beaumont. He had given it to her with a sacred oath that she had stolen his heart, and he would be forever hers. Their families had been enemies, but eventually the young lovers found their happiness. The ring had been passed down through the generations until its sale at an auction. The letters and other items of provenance were available should Liam wish to purchase them. He had, and they rested in the box with the ring.

Rising to his feet, he ambled across to the wooden chest, opened it up, and lifting out the small, red velvet box, he stared at the precious piece of jewelry. Carrying it back to his chair, he slumped down, placed it on the table next to him, picked up his phone and called Marie.

"Hi, Liam. Did you forget something?"

"In a manner of speakin'. I need your advice."

"Why do I think this is about the girl who's stolen your heart?"

Her words hit him.

Stolen your heart?

Coincidence!

It was a common phrase!

"Liam?"

"Sorry, Marie. Yeah, it's Summer. She has a channel on YouTube. I don't know what to do."

"You've lost me."

"If I watch it and she's mediocre—"

"It won't matter," she said cutting him off, "but if she's fabulous, you'll be all over the place. Represent her, don't represent her, and so on."

"Correct."

"Liam, you're overthinking this. If she's great, you'll figure it out."

"Maybe, but you know how I feel about blurred lines. How the hell would I manage a woman I'm involved with?"

"The way you'd manage any other artist."

"Fuck."

"Why are you so worried about this?"

"I don't want anything to mess things up. I really—uh—like this girl."

"Oops. It almost slipped out."

"Marie, would you please stick to the point?" he snapped, totally unnerved about what he'd almost said.

"Sure. Liam, you are more than capable of handling a young woman who gets too big for her britches."

He paused.

She was right.

He still felt queasy.

"Do me a favor. Go watch her and call me back."

"You're kidding?"

"Call me back and tell me if she's okay, good, or better than good. Oh, and one more thing. I don't know how many songs she's got up there, but look for one called, One-Way Street."

"Is this my brother I'm talking to? The self-made, self-assured, take-no prisoners guy that—"

"Marie, just do it."

"Ah, there he is. Thank God. Okay. I'll get right back to you."

Ending the call, he picked up the ring and studied the majestic ruby. As the fire's flickering brought it to life, he couldn't stop asking himself if it meant to grace Summer's finger.

"Fuck. I barely know the girl," he muttered under his breath. "Maybe there'll be a sign, or I'll have a flash, or maybe she'll say something, or...dammit, what the hell is wrong with me? Too much damn cognac, that's what's wrong with me."

Putting the ring back in its box, he closed the lid and returned it to the chest, but as he ambled back to his chair his phone rang.

Marie.

His heart skipped.

Striding the last few steps, he anxiously answered the call.

"Tell me!"

"Liam, you need to watch it."

"That doesn't tell me anything," he said briskly, dropping back into his chair.

"Let me put it like this. If you don't sign her and her band, I'll have Eric draw up papers and start my own management company. That's how good she is. No, that's how great she is."

"Fuck. I knew it."

"Liam, I don't swear, but she is eff'ing unbelievable."

"Wait. She has a band?"

"Not like a regular band. She has a pianist who's absolutely fantastic. I assume that's her brother you mentioned. There's also a sax player that will knock your socks off, but she...holy smokes."

"Why did I know this?" he grunted.

"Because that's what you do, remember? You could walk into a bar and point to someone and say, that guy can sing. Trust me. Watch it! I'm off to bed."

"No! Wait for me to call you back."

"Jeez, Liam."

"Please."

"Okay."

Quickly moving to his desk, he picked up his seventeen-inch Powerbook, took it back to his chair, had another sip of Dutch courage, then opened it up and entered a search on YouTube for Summer Sings - A One-Way Street. A moment later she came to life on his screen, standing beside the piano in her parents' living room with Harry seated behind her. He began to play, a saxophone joined in, then faded into the background, and Summer's smoky, bluesy, uniquely toned voice lifted into the air.

Life is a road we travel each day
Why am I always losing my way?
I miss the green light, I stop and I wait
Where do I turn? Is it all up to fate?
I've crashed a few times, no bruises to show
Other times I've sat and let tears freely flow
The aches and cuts heal, but the scars remain
And each time I see you I remember the pain.
Cos you have the power to turn my tears into rain.
My tears into rain.
Love is lonely on a one-way street.
You're always ahead, how can we meet?
Love is hopeless on a one-way street
It burns in my chest with a white hot heat.
Life sends me forward, I can't turn back
I look over my shoulder, did I lose track?
Miles, like time, zip by me so fast
Will I leave you behind, lost in my past?
You look but don't see me
You listen but don't hear me
There's no love lost cos no love has been found
I'm invisible because you won't turn around.
Living on hope, it can feel so empty
Will you become just another memory?
Should I exit now, before it's too late?
Or should I keep dreaming, should I still wait?
Love is lonely on a one-way street.
You're always ahead, how can we meet?
Love is hopeless on a one-way street
And it burns in my chest with a white hot heat.

Love is lonely on a one-way street.
Love is sad on a one-way street
Love is forsaken on a one-way street
Still it burns in my chest with a white hot heat.
Each time I see you I remember the pain.
Cos you have the power to turn my tears into rain.
My tears into rain.
My tears into rain.
You have the power to turn my tears into rain.
Part the clouds, and let the sun dry the pain.

The last line floated in the air like mist, and Liam realized he was holding his breath. The melody was haunting, the piano had Harry's unique combination of chords and changes, the saxophone had drawn him with its sensuality, but Summer's voice...it possessed a depth and a rare richness. Her pitch was perfect, and her control was like that of a seasoned performer.

But she had something else, something even more compelling.

She had exposed her heart and oozed raw emotion.

She hadn't written the song to audition it for him.

She had written it about him, about how she felt.

A Song For Liam

There was tightness in his chest, and closing his eyes he sucked in the air, then finally picking up his phone he called his sister.

"So? Was I right?"

"She's insanely good. She's like, I don't know, I'd say Adele meets Jewel, but that's not giving Summer the credit she deserves. She's one-hundred percent absolutely unique."

"I totally agree, Liam, and who was playing the sax?"

"I have no idea."

"She gave me chills. Summer's a star. It's only a matter of time before someone see's her and—"

"I know. It'll be like Justin Bieber. Marie, what do I do?"

"Just be who you are! Jeez, Liam, grow a pair! I'm going to bed. Love you, and congrats! You've done it again...assuming you do!"

She was gone.

He stared at his phone.

Did his sister just say grow a pair?

"Holy shit. She's right!" he exclaimed. "What the hell?"

Returning to his computer, he watched the video again. The song was a hit, of that he had no doubt, and Summer was going to be a huge star. All he needed to do now was tell her, but when had she written A Song For Liam?

"Dammit," he grunted. "Jump in. Just jump in, but I don't wanna call her and say, hey, Summer, I'm gonna sign you. No, it has to be...what? Different! But how? Shit."

Rising to his feet, he walked over to his window and stared at the rain.

He missed her.

He missed her like crazy.

Suddenly he knew exactly when to tell her, and he knew exactly how. Feeling as if he was living some kind of surreal, lucid dream, he marched back to his phone, snatched it up, and called her. She answered immediately.

"Liam? Hey."

"Did I wake you? You sound sleepy."

"I'm just laying here in the dark missing you."

"I'm missin' you too, sugar. How's your butt?"

"Liam!"

"Answer the question."

"A bit tender."

"Hmmm. Just a bit? Sounds like it needs more attention."

"Oh well, such is life. It'll just have to wait until you decide to get back here."

"I have a better idea. What would you say about you and Harry jumpin' on my jet and joinin' me for New Year's?"

"Say that to me again—slowly."

"You heard me."

"Holy crap. Do you mean it? Seriously?"

"Yeah, of course I mean it."

"Oh! My! God! Liam!"

"Is that a yes?"

"What do you think? Oh, my gosh, oh my gosh, oh my gosh."

"When you tell your parents in the mornin', tell your dad, Liam says you're welcome."

"I don't understand."

"You don't have to. He will."

"Liam, thank you! I can't believe it, and I can't wait to see you."

"Back at ya, sugar. Be sure to pack enough for a few days. Harry can leave whenever he wants, but you've gotta stick around."

"You won't get any arguments from me."

"You know what'll happen if I do! I'm gonna go now. I've gotta crazy few days ahead, but I'll call you tomorrow with all the details."

"Okay. Wow. Thanks again. Goodnight, Liam."

* * *

Ending the call, Summer closed her eyes and hugged herself.

"Please, Dear God, keep the weather nice. What am I saying? I'm going no matter what."

CHAPTER SIXTEEN
December 31st

The days following Liam's departure had been a whirlwind of activity for Summer and her family. It had started the morning she announced the exciting news that she and Harry had been invited to Liam's party, and would be flown to Nashville in his private jet. Her mother had declared she was taking them into the huge shopping mall in the next county to buy them new outfits for the big event.

"We can cruise the after-Christmas sales," she'd exclaimed. "Did Liam say if it was formal? You need to find out. Will Harry need a tux?"

Liam assured Summer Harry didn't need a tux, but something snappy wouldn't be amiss. The shopping had lasted all day, and by the time they'd arrived home Summer had been worn out. She'd eaten dinner, carefully put away her new clothes, and after a brief conversation with Liam, she'd worked on her new song until she'd been unable to keep her eyes open.

But the focus abruptly shifted to Liam's house.

The men from the county met Keith, Summer, and Ted Duncan, the contractor who had renovated the home, at Liam's house. Summer had stood in the cold listening to endless conversations, but the house had been cleared for entry.

The following morning she and her father had returned to meet up with the same group of people, but Harry had joined them. Hard hats were distributed, and they ventured inside. The floors were strewn with pictures and objects that had fallen from their shelves or off the wall, but it appeared the front of the house had suffered little damage. Entering Liam's den, she had been overjoyed to find it still intact.

Still in possession of Liam's keys, she'd made her way to the locked door at the end of the hall. Opening it up, she'd switched on her powerful flashlight and stepped carefully down the stairs. To her great relief the studio appeared to be undamaged, but hearing her father urgently call her name, she hurried back up. She found him in the hall wearing a deep frown."

"Prepare yourself," he'd said solemnly, guiding her to the back of the house. "This isn't pretty."

A boulder had plowed through the upstairs back wall into the master bedroom, then crashed through the floor and into the kitchen. Staring at the massive rock, then looking up through the huge hole into the room where she and Liam had been sleeping, a chill shuddered through her body.

But for her vision, they would not have survived.

Seeing how shaken she was, Keith had taken her outside, but Ted had joined them a few minutes later to call Liam. It had been a long and detailed conversation, then Ted had handed Summer his phone.

"Liam. The rock. It's unbelievable."

"Yeah, so I gathered. Ted promised to send me pictures. Summer, I've given this a lotta thought and I've decided to rebuild." Then pausing, he added, "You saved us both."

"I might have had the vision, but I can't take credit for it. I don't know where it came from."

"You must have an angel on your shoulder."

The only glitch to the day was Harry's disappearance. He'd wandered off into the adjacent forest through which Liam and Summer had made their escape. Keith was about to send out a search party when he'd finally reappeared.

But now the drama of entering Liam's house was behind her, and sitting in the sumptuous Gulf Stream G550, Summer's heart thumped against her chest. She was suddenly living a fairytale, but her racing pulse wasn't just because of the thrilling trip. Liam's New Year's Eve party would be filled with glamorous celebrities. How could she possibly measure up?

Was her dress pretty enough?

Elegant enough?

Sexy enough?

She was just a small town girl. What did she know about sipping champagne from crystal glasses and making chit-chat with the rich and famous?

"Are you gonna take all day?" Harry asked, interrupting her thoughts. "Aren't you dyin' of curiosity? It's bulky. There has to be more inside than just the invitation."

When she and Harry had stepped into the plane, they'd found gold envelopes bearing their names sitting on the first two seats.

"I was thinking about, uh, stuff," she muttered.

"How can you stand it? Screw it, I'm openin' mine."

"You didn't have to wait for me."

"I felt like I did."

"Sometimes you can be very sweet, Harry. Let's open them together."

The flap was sealed with black wax, the letters LT plain to see. Peeling it back, she peered inside. The embossed invitation had come with a gold chain, hanging from which was a rolled gold number twenty, encrusted with sparkling stones.

"Whoa. I guess we're official," Harry said staring at it, "but I'll feel a bit weird wearin' a necklace."

"I suspect it's some kind of honor," Summer remarked, staring at the glossy, sparkling jewelry, wondering if she was looking at real diamonds. "Like a gold medal."

"You think so?"

"I do. I just found a note. Keep this with you. L&K, Liam."

"I have one too, but it doesn't say L&K. What does that mean?"

"Uh, love and kisses, I guess."

"Good grief," Harry muttered, rolling his eyes. "I'm gonna check out the rest of this plane."

"Go ahead. I just want to sit here for a minute."

As Harry walked away to explore, Summer stared around the luxurious cabin. Though she didn't want to admit it, she found the prospect of flying in the small aircraft nerve-racking, but watching Harry's uninhibited delight made her smile. Moving her gaze out the window, she couldn't believe she was actually there.

The week had sailed past.

She'd soon be where she belonged.

In Liam's arms.

"Hey, Summer!"

Startled, she turned around and saw Harry opening and closing the panel separating the compartments.

"Check it out. Cool, huh?"

Memories from her morning with Liam flashed through her mind.

"Harry, please don't," she exclaimed, her face blushing red. "You'll break something."

"Not to worry," Frank said, stepping into the cabin and moving towards them, "but you do need to take a seat and buckle up. We'll be taking off shortly. Once we level out you can help yourself to whatever you want in the galley, but when you sit back down, please make sure to fasten your seat belt."

"Can I see inside the cockpit?" Harry asked eagerly.

Breaking into a smile, Frank shook his head.

"Not this trip, but when we land I'll check with Mr. Taylor and see what he says about letting you upfront for the return. Ah, here's Stewart Masters. He's my right hand. Stewart, this is Summer and Harry Brown."

"Hi, good to meet you," the copilot said with a happy grin. "I'll see you in there, Frank."

"Um...I'm a bit nervous," Summer said softly. "I know I shouldn't be, but I am. This plane is so small."

"It feels a whole lot different from a commercial jet, but most people get used to it fairly quickly. This will be a relatively short flight. It's good for your first time. I was a commercial pilot for a while, and I much prefer flying a plane like this."

"You do?"

"Definitely. I'm going up front now. Make sure your seat belts are buckled. I'll let you know when it's okay to get up and move around."

She watched him walk away and disappear into the cockpit, then looked over at Harry.

"You're so calm."

"Says who?" Harry shot back, his eyes wide. "I'm scared shitless, but it's so cool."

"Yeah, it is. I just wish my heart would stop pounding."

"Hey, Summer, guess who called me?"

"I have no idea, Harry. Who called you?"

"Crystal Blake."

"The name rings a vague bell."

"You know, the girl back in high-school I was so nuts about who was going out with Robbie Parker."

"That stuck-up cheerleader who made fun of you because you played classical music?"

"Yeah, and Melissa Simons called too, and that cute girl at Starbucks gave me a latte for free yesterday."

"Suddenly you're a ladies man. Why do you think that is, Harry?"

"Well, duh!" he retorted. "Because they must have heard I'm goin' to Liam Taylor's New Year's Eve party on his private jet."

"I think that's a pretty good—shit—Harry, we're moving."

"This is so cool!"

"So you keep saying, but that's okay, keep talking. It'll help. Please, Harry, keep talking."

"Are you shittin' me? I don't even remember what I was sayin'."

As the jet rolled down the runway Summer gripped the armrests, but Harry started chuckling, and when it lifted off the ground, his nervous merriment became contagious. Summer suddenly broke into peals of hysteria.

"I don't know what's so funny," Summer said breathlessly, still laughing out loud. "Why am I like this?"

"Maybe sheer terror?" Harry suggested. "Holy crap!"

"Oh, my gosh! This is unfucking believable."

"I know I complain about you sometimes, but right now I'm really glad you're my sister."

"Harry—I need a drink. Like, a serious drink."

"You and me both!"

* * *

Eagerly awaiting Summer's arrival, Liam stood in the elegantly decorated banquet room of The Hermitage Hotel. Built in 1910, it reeked of old-world charm and sophistication. The building had been renovated in 2000, but with its domed ceilings and archways the feel of yesteryear was still alive. Liam sometimes thought he was an old soul. He was drawn to bygone eras, and had a passion for antiques.

"Any other notes, Mr. Taylor?"

The question had come from Benny, the tech supervising the evening's entertainment.

"Just make sure there's not a peep before starting the last feature. I want the drama of the moment."

"Will do."

"Thanks, Benny. I've gotta run, but feel free to call if anything crops up."

It was time to head to the airport, and Liam didn't want to be late. Stopping briefly at the reception desk, he double-checked the arrangements he'd made for Harry's accommodation, and picked up the key. It was a Deluxe King, and while Liam was sure Harry would be blown away by the sumptuous room, he would find the minibar held no alcohol.

An invitation to Liam Taylor's New Year's Eve party was the hottest ticket in Nashville, but being a celebrity was not a requirement, and being a guest one year did not automatically ensure your attendance the next.

But Liam held a second party.

The creme-de-la-creme of Nashville's New Year's Eve gatherings.

It was his private gathering for a select few in the Presidential Suite.

Summer's assumption had been correct.

Receiving the pendant was considered an honor.

It was the invitation to the elite gathering in the Presidential Suite.

Boasting a sumptuous buffet, a full bar with a skilled mixologist, and the very best French champagne, the select lucky few enjoyed an evening in quiet luxury, but with freedom to join in the boisterous celebration in the banquet room.

The Presidential Suite was also where Liam spent the night.

Though he'd always looked forward to a roll between the sheets with the beautiful woman who happened to be at his side, the thought of spending the special evening with Summer sent his pulse racing.

Walking outside and settling into the back seat of the waiting limousine, he pulled out his phone and went to work. Spending the drive deep in conversation, and sending quick responses to texts and emails, he was soon climbing out and moving briskly into the private terminal.

Catching sight of Summer walking towards him, his heart leapt.

"Hey, sugar," he called happily, opening his arms.

In spite of the thousand and one details that had been running through his mind, as she fell against him and he wrapped her up, he suddenly had only two thoughts.

The ruby ring, and A Song For Liam.

CHAPTER SEVENTEEN

For the first few minutes, the drive from the airport back to the hotel was oddly quiet. Summer had looped her arm through Liam's elbow and was blissfully leaning against him, while Harry had stared out the window engrossed by the sights.

"Are you guys tired, or gearin' up for tonight," Liam finally asked.

"I think Harry's a bit shell-shocked," Summer said, winking at her brother.

"I am not. I'm just lookin' at everything."

Summer's phone chimed snatching her attention. Rummaging through her bag, she pulled it out and checked the caller.

"Shoot, It's dad. I promised I'd let him know when we landed and I forgot," she muttered. "Hi, dad. We just landed a few minutes ago."

"Good flight?"

"Amazing."

"Is Liam with you?"

"Yes, he's right here. Do you need him?"

"Sure do."

"Dad wants to talk to you," Summer said, handing Liam the phone.

"Hi Keith. Happy New Year. What's up?"

"I just got a phone call from a limo company askin' what time they should pick us up."

"Oh, that."

"Yeah, that."

"I thought it would be nice to have a bottle of wine and not worry about drivin' home."

"Liam, it's—"

"An early anniversary present," Liam declared, finishing the sentence, "and a thank you for bein' at my house and dealin' with the red tape and my contractor. Have a great night, and give Janet my love. I'm puttin' Summer back on the phone."

"Hey dad."

"That man of yours ordered a limo for your mother and me. What a thoughtful guy."

"He did?" she exclaimed, looking up at Liam with a grateful grin. "I hope you two have a super time, and Happy New Year. I'll call you tomorrow."

"Not early, we're sleepin' in."

"I promise. Bye."

"Bye, kitten."

"Liam, that was so generous," she said gratefully, dropping the phone back inside her bag.

"What was?" Harry asked. "What did I miss?"

"Liam arranged a limo for mom and dad tonight."

"I've gotta stay in good with them so I can keep seein' their daughter."

"Hah. That's funny, Liam," Harry said with a chuckle. "Um, by the way, you mentioned your house."

"What about it?"

"You own the land around it, right?"

"About twenty acres. It extends across the wooded area along the side."

"That's what I thought."

"Why do you ask?"

"I took a wander over there yesterday and I found a huge area of flat land, probably about two acres. It looks like an old buildin' pad, and I can understand why. It would have a helluva view once the brush was cleared away."

"What are you suggestin', Harry?"

"The back of your house is totally wrecked. Maybe you should demolish it completely, renovate the area that survived, and turn it into a guest house for your musicians. Summer said the basement studio wasn't damaged at all."

"Yeah, keep goin.'"

"Then build a new home on the pad I found. There's no steep peak behind it, and surrounded by forest you'll have a whole lot more privacy. Where your house is now is great, but it's exposed. Anyone drivin' up that road can see it through the gates."

"Damn, Harry, that's a great idea. I've always wanted to design my own home."

"I don't think it'll take long to repair the front of your house," Harry continued. "You could stay there while your new place is bein' built."

"Why didn't you tell me your little brother was so smart, Summer?"

"He's surprising me too," she said with a grin. "I mean, seriously, who are you, and what did you do with Harry?"

"I owe you for this," Liam said gratefully. "I'm gonna send my contractor an email tomorrow to check out that site, and Harry, I'm gonna find a special way to thank you for this brainstorm of yours."

"You can fly me around in that jet any time you want," Harry said eagerly. "I've never been in a small plane before. It was so cool."

"I know what you mean. You can sense the speed, especially on take-off and landin'. Kinda feels like you're in a rocket ship."

"It totally does. I can't wait to tell Crystal."

"Is that your girlfriend?"

"Are you kidding?" Summer chimed in. "In high-school Harry was a nerd who locked himself in the music room for hours, and Crystal was a cheerleader who wouldn't give him the time of day. Now she's calling him, along with every other girl in town."

"Not every other girl," Harry retorted, but with a wicked grin. "Just a few."

"Harry, I'm gonna make a suggestion," Liam said. "The gold pendant you found with your invitation means you're a special guest. There's only a handful of people who receive one, and it gets you through the door of the Presidential Suite into a private party."

"Cool. Thanks, Liam."

"Havin' it around your neck is gonna bring you attention. People are gonna wanna know who you are, especially unattached females.

"No kiddin'?"

"Actually, even some of the attached ones," Liam added with a wink, "but you wanna be careful with them. The point is, it's better not to wear it at first. If you see a girl you wanna talk to, approach her. If she gives you the cold shoulder, so be it. If she's nice back, then great, she likes you. Sounds to me Crystal isn't interested in you, she's interested in what's happenin' in your life and wants to be a part of it."

"Yeah, but it's cool," Harry muttered, a devilish grin curling his lips. "It's like dad said. You'll get your chance to get even, you might just have to wait a bit. I think my waitin' is about done."

"Harry!" Summer exclaimed, shocked at her brother's confession. "Oh, Harry, you are so bad."

"In spite of how you see me, I'm not twelve anymore, and Summer, I'm not a complete moron."

"Did you just let me sit here and give you unnecessary advice?" Liam said with a laugh. "Summer's right, you are bad."

"No, no," Harry said hastily. "I just didn't wanna be rude, and I do appreciate the advice. I probably would have draped that thing around me without thinkin', then realized what I'd done and been ticked off."

"Hey, Harry, don't panic, it's all good," Liam assured him, still chuckling.

"I still don't believe it," Summer muttered. "I'll ask you again, what happened to my little brother?"

"I grew up a while back, you just didn't notice."

"Good, we're here," Liam declared as the car turned into the hotel. "We'll be stayin' overnight, then goin' to my home tomorrow. You've got your own room, Harry. I'll take you there first, and then upstairs so you'll know where the Presidential Suite is. That's were Summer and I will be."

"Liam, thanks again for includin' me in all this. It's awesome."

"You're welcome. I'm glad you could join us."

After explaining to the chauffeur which bags went to which rooms, Liam led Harry and Summer into the hotel and across to the elevators, but Summer's head was spinning.

The hotel was even grander than she'd expected, and a wave of fresh nerves took hold. Though she and Harry weren't completely sheltered, and Liam's Apple Valley home was far from run-of-the-mill, neither of them had stayed in a place as luxurious as The Hermitage.

"This is incredible," Harry breathed as they entered his room. "It makes me feel like I'm a somebody."

"You are a somebody," Liam replied, his voice suddenly solemn. "Harry, very few people have a gift like yours. It won't happen overnight, but your music will take you places, you can count on it."

"Uh, if you say so."

"Let's go upstairs. I'll show you where the suite is."

"So—they'll just drop off my bag?"

"Yep, it'll be here when you get back."

As they headed out, Summer curled her fingers around Liam's hand. She knew Harry was talented, but Liam thought Harry was something special, and she couldn't help but feel a twinge of jealously.

"Are you okay, Summer?" Liam asked, sensing a change in her mood.

"Yes, fine, great," she lied. "Just a bit overwhelmed by all this."

"You'll love staying in the suite. It's has everything you could ever want, and more."

She wanted to say, all I want is you, but thinking it would sound too hokey she bit her tongue, and though she'd seen the pictures of the Presidential Suite on the hotel's website, when Liam opened the door, she caught her breath.

"It's another world," she murmured, moving slowly forward, then seeing her garment bag draped across the back of a chair, her heart sank.

The burgundy dress with the beaded collar she'd bought on sale at a trendy boutique seemed completely inadequate.

So did the new satin shoes.

And her hair.

Everything was wrong.

It was all horribly wrong.

"Harry, why don't you explore the hotel," Liam suggested, seeing the expression on Summer's face. "I'll call you in a little while and let you know the plan for tonight."

"Yeah, sure. See you soon, Summer."

"Have fun, Harry."

* * *

Waiting until Harry closed the door behind him, Liam stepped up to Summer, placed his hands on her shoulders, and turned her around to face him.

"Hey, what's the matter?"

"I'm sorry," she whispered, "I just feel..."

"You just feel what?"

"I don't know where to begin."

"Come with me," he said, taking her hand and leading her across the room. "We're gonna have a lie down. You need to relax."

"What a good idea. I'd like that very much."

Entering the bedroom and kicking off his shoes, he watched her remove her jacket and unzip her boots. She looked almost depressed, and he hoped he hadn't said or done something to upset her.

"Okay, sugar," he murmured, pulling her into his arms as they stretched out on the king-sized bed, "tell me what's goin' on. Whatever it is, I promise I'll do my best to fix it."

"This is embarrassing, but, uh, I bought a new dress and it won't be good enough. It won't even come close."

"Hey, sugar, you could wear a burlap sack, and you'd still be the prettiest girl in the room."

"That's nice of you to say, but we both know everyone will be in designer gowns that cost thousands of dollars, but it's not just the dress. I won't fit in. I'll let you down."

"I'll tell you a little story," he began, hugging her tightly. "When I went to my first Grammy party I was scared shitless. I stood in front of the mirror changin' ties, then tryin' bolero's, thinkin' nothin' I did was right, but as it turned out, no-one gave a rat's ass. It didn't take me long to realize they were too worried about themselves to care about me and my clothes."

"It's different for guys."

"Not as much as you think, and we're always tryin' to catch the eye of gorgeous girls like you. Sure, there will be women there in expensive outfits, but you'll look incredible whatever you're wearin'."

"You can't possibly know that."

"Sure I can. You're so damn beautiful, you'll turn every head in the place, and Sugar, they're gonna love your dress because I'm gonna love your dress, and I'll make sure that's obvious."

"Thank you for saying all that, but I know I won't measure up, and I want you to be proud of me."

Liam wanted to kick himself.

He'd brought her from a small town to attend a Nashville party filled with celebrities. At the very least, he should have told her he'd have an outfit waiting, and made sure it was a dress that would make her feel like a princess.

"Sorry, Liam," she mumbled hastily. "I'm really thrilled to be here, but I'm a pack of nerves."

"I'm gonna make you a promise," he said solemnly, shifting to catch her eye. "By the end of tonight, all these insecurities you're feelin' will be history."

"Can you hit the fast forward button and make me feel that way now?"

"Unfortunately, that particular button on my superpower suit is out for repair, but I am gonna make you forget about all your worries. I've been achin' for you every single minute since I left Apple Valley."

"Liam...I've missed you so much."

Smoothing a stray hair from her face, he pressed his lips on hers, slowly unfastened the buttons on her thick, woolen cardigan, then moving his mouth to her neck, he tongued his way down to her bra-covered breasts.

"I've gotta get these dang jeans off," he suddenly grunted, rolling off the bed.

As he hurriedly stripped and retrieved a condom from the night-stand drawer, Summer pulled off her slacks and underwear.

"It's so good to be naked with you," he purred, climbing on top of her. "Damn, girl, I love your body."

Returning his lips to her breasts, she moaned loudly, raising her chest as he hungrily drew in her nipples.

"Baby you are so wet," he growled, slipping his fingers into her pussy. "I wanna take you back to my place and do wicked things to you."

"Like what?"

"You wanna hear?"

"Desperately," she panted, wriggling against his touch.

"Wrap your body in rope, suck on your titty tops until you're squealin', then flog your beautiful backside. I wanna bend you over a bench, tie your legs apart and tease you for an hour...and that's just for starters."

"Liam...please..."

"Please, what?" he whispered, his breath tickling her ear. "You're not gettin' it 'til you ask real nice."

"Please, Liam, please slide your cock inside me."

"Then what?"

"Fuck me. Please, fuck me."

"Are you beggin'?" he pressed, moving his hand from her pussy and pinching the inside of her thighs. "I'm not doin' it until you're beggin'."

"Yes, I am, I'm begging," she bleated. "I swear, I am."

"Do you believe you're gonna be the prettiest girl in the room? Are you gonna hold your head up high? Do you promise to remember I'm nuts about you, and so dang proud of you I can't hardly stand it?"

"Yes, yes, I promise."

Resting his weight on top of her, he pushed her legs apart with his, lifted his hips, and taking hold of his member, he placed it against her pussy and plunged home. Letting out a deep, grateful groan, she threw her hands above her head.

"Hold me down? Please, hold me down?"

Her unbridled need for his dominance sent his blood pumping. Gripping her wrists and thrusting with strong, slow strokes, her mewling whimpers and desperate writhing fed the fever overtaking him. Diving his mouth to her lips in a crushing kiss, he quickened his pace. Her muffled cries spurred him on, and as she threw her legs around his waist, he raised his head and stared down at her. As if sensing his gaze, she opened her crystal blue eyes. He could see her need, her hunger, and her lust.

"Liam," she whispered, "I love this so much."

"Me too, baby, more than you can know."

Straightening up and grabbing her ankles, he deftly flipped her over, then grasped her hips and pulled her into his pelvis.

"Your ass is way too pale," he declared, landing several hot smacks.

Though letting out a squeal, she wriggled as if asking for more. He obliged, delivering a volley of stinging slaps, then sliding back inside her, he gave into his urgent need, pumping without pause until he felt himself on the edge.

"Liam," she panted as he slowed, "please don't stop. I'm so close."

He tightened his grip.

"You ready?" he growled. "I'm about to fuck you hard."

"Yes, yes, I'm ready, I swear."

He immediately began pummeling her pussy, increasing the force and vigor of his strokes as he feasted his eyes on her reddened backside.

She suddenly arched her back and let out a wail.

Her orgasm sent him over the edge, and there was no stopping his powerful climax. Sucking in the air, he surrendered to the fierce convulsions shuddering through his loins.

* * *

A few minutes later, entwined in each other's arms, Summer let out a long, contented sigh.

"Liam, I'm sorry I got all weird on you."

"You've got nothin' to apologize for. I'm the one who's sorry. I'm an idiot sometimes."

"I have no idea what you're talking about, but, uh, can I show you the dress?"

"I'd love to see it."

"But you have to promise you'll tell me if it's not right. Don't say you like it if you don't."

"I promise."

"The garment bag is in the other room. I'll be right back?"

Slipping from his arms, she pulled on her thick cardigan and disappeared through the door. Sitting up and waiting for her return, he wished he could convey how little the dress mattered. Being on his arm would make her the envy of every woman there.

"Here it is," she said nervously, walking back in and holding it up for his inspection.

"Sugar, what's not to like? I love the color, and I love the beads and rhinestones around the neckline," he declared, meaning every word. "Dang, girl, that dress looks like it was made for you. I can't wait to see you wearin' it and—whoa!"

"And whoa?"

"I, uh, I've gotta make a call, but trust me, it's the most perfect dress you could possibly wear, and you're gonna find out just how perfect real soon."

CHAPTER EIGHTEEN

Summer stared at her reflection. Thanks to Liam's fervent reassurances, she thought the sensuous burgundy dress looked even lovelier than it had in the boutique.

It was sleeveless, and fanned out from a pearl and sparkling rhinestone collar to a form-fitting bodice, flowing into a floor length, full skirt. A matching beaded sash encircled her waist highlighting her figure, and the low back was just as eye-catching with crisscrossing straps.

Using her curling iron she had rolled her long, straight hair into flowing waves, then pulled back one side with a burgundy rhinestone comb. Smoky grey eyeshadow, black mascara, and a dark red lipgloss made the picture almost complete. The final touch was the diamond and ruby tennis bracelet her parents had given her for her twenty-first birthday. Hearing a gentle tap, she walked across the spacious bedroom and opened the door expecting to see Liam, but Harry grinned back at her.

"Holy cow, Summer. You look like you belong in a magazine."

"Thanks, Harry, and you don't look so bad yourself. I wasn't sure when you put that outfit together, but now I am. You're tall enough to carry off that long jacket, and that silver bolero against that dark green shirt really jumps out. You'll be batting the girls away with a stick."

"I prefer to reel them in."

"Very funny."

"Where's Liam? He said to meet you guys here at eight-thirty."

"He stepped out, but there he is," she said, seeing Liam enter the room over Harry's shoulder. "I'm very happy to see you, Mr. Taylor," she declared, stepping forward to meet him. "You've been gone so long I thought I'd lost you."

"Not a chance, and you look...wow...I'm speechless."

"I'm acceptable?"

"You'd outglam the actresses at the Oscars."

"You clean up pretty good yourself," she remarked, eyeing his flashy suit and skinny purple bowtie. "Where did you change?"

"In the other bedroom. I wanted to give you plenty of space. Harry, I'm gonna steal your sister for a minute."

"Sure, go ahead. Can I help myself to that buffet over there? I'm starvin.'"

"That's what it's there for."

"Cool. Can I have a beer?"

"One," Summer said firmly. "Pace yourself."

"Yeah, I know all about that."

"Famous last words," she muttered.

As Harry walked away, Liam guided Summer back into the bedroom and closed the door.

"Don't worry about Harry," he assured her. "I have someone watchin' over him. If he tries to order any of the hard stuff he'll hit a brick wall name Sam, and the limit for Harry tonight is three beers."

"Thank you. That's a relief. I wasn't quite sure how to handle that. I've never seen him drink heavily, but he could get loaded at college and we'd have no idea."

"He probably does. It's a rite of passage."

"I guess. Is that what you wanted to tell me, or is there something else?"

"Uh, yeah, there's something else."

"Why do you look so serious? Is there a problem?"

"What? Lord no. It's...the thing is..."

"Liam, you're starting to freak me out."

"Sorry. I have something for you. Uh, let's sit down."

Taking her hand and leading her to the couch beneath the window, as they sat down, he ran his fingers through his hair, then cleared his throat.

"Liam, what's wrong with you?"

"Nothin', I'm just trying to figure out how to, uh, do this."

"Do what?"

"Explain about what I have for you."

"Why don't you start at the beginning?"

"Yeah, good suggestion. Okay, let's see. A few years back I was in England, and I took off by myself to explore the countryside. I was off the beaten track in the middle of nowhere and I stumbled across this antique shop, and when I say antique shop, I mean the real deal. Anyway, I found something there, something special, and I, uh, the thing is..."

"You're giving me something you found in an antique store in England? Oh, my gosh."

"Just wait a second."

"Sorry, but this is kind of nerve-racking."

"No kiddin'," he muttered under his breath. "As I was sayin', the thing is, I want you to know—I need you to know—how special you are to me," he continued, his voice falling soft as he pulled the burgundy velvet box from his pocket. "I've missed you like crazy these last few days, so, anyway, here, I want you to have this."

A ring box was the last thing Summer had expected, and as she took it between her fingers, a wave of goosebumps pricked her skin. Trying to calm herself, she slowly pushed up the lid, then gasped as she gazed at the ruby ring.

"Liam...it's...it's...so beautiful, and it matches my dress, it even matches my bracelet."

"I didn't know about the bracelet, I knew about the dress. When you showed it to me earlier, I swear, I felt like I was bein' told to go home and get that ring and bring it back here for you. I didn't have to as it turned out. My sister picked it up for me. Sorry, I don't know why I told you all that," he said, shaking his head, thinking he'd just been babbling like an idiot.

"I'm totally blown away. It's gorgeous. I've never seen anything like it."

"It dates back to the 17th century. I had it researched and found out it belonged to a Countess named Victoria Beaumont."

Darting her head up, she stared at him with wide eyes.

"Why are you lookin' like that?"

"That's my middle name. Victoria."

"Say, what?"

"Summer Victoria Brown."

He was about to speak, but a chill rattled through his body.

"This is really weird, Liam. It's wonderful, but it's really weird."

"Yeah, it is."

"What do you make of it?"

"All I know is, the minute I laid eyes on that ring I had to have it," then pausing to take a breath, he lowered his voice. "I knew it was gonna be for the woman I...uh...the woman I was gonna love, and that's you, Summer. There, I've said it. Sorry, I made a total mess of that," he mumbled, running his fingers through his hair again.

Rarely did he feel out of his depth, but suddenly he did, and it was embarrassing.

"You didn't make a mess of anything," she breathed. "This is amazing. The ring is amazing, and I'm crazy in love with you too. You know that, right? I have been for ages."

"I told you earlier, I'm nuts about you, and I was drawn to you from that first day you knocked on my door," he said huskily, and holding her face between his hands, he pressed his lips against hers, hoping she could feel the raw emotion sweeping through his heart.

"Liam, I feel like I'm living a dream, the best dream I could ever have."

"Yeah, it does kinda feel like that, and I need to tell you more about the ring."

"Oh, please do. I want to know everything."

"It was given to Victoria by her lover. Oh, I should tell you, she was a countess and he was an earl. Anyway, they couldn't be together because their families were enemies and he wanted her to know that he loved her, and that he'd find a way for them to be together."

"That's so romantic. Do you know if they were? Ultimately together, I mean."

"Yep, they got there in the end. Summer, I wanna give it to you as my promise. I'm totally committed to you, and I want us to be together. I want you to wear it and never take it off. If we reach that, uh, next step, then, uh, I'll go shoppin' and—"

"Stop," she said, cutting him off. "If we reach that next step, this ring will go from being a promise ring to an engagement ring. Yikes, I can't believe I said that."

"Hey, I love that idea. It's perfect. Let's see if it fits."

Lifting it from the box, Summer tried to place it on the middle finger of her left hand, but it was too small.

She paused, then slowly raised her eyes.

"We could have it sized," she murmured.

"Nope, try it on your ring finger. It's okay, go ahead."

Feeling her pulse tick up, she took a breath, then did as he asked.

It slipped perfectly into place.

"I knew it," he murmured. "That ring is exactly where it belongs."

"I feel all funny," she said breathlessly. "Like, really emotional and unbelievably happy. I feel like I'm going to burst."

"Yeah, me too."

"So, what now?"

"Now it needs to be sealed with another kiss, and something else. Something to keep you warm and toasty."

"Why do I think I'm about to get my ass spanked?"

"Just enough to seal the deal, and help you through the night."

"But I'm all dressed, and neat and tidy, and my hair's perfect."

"Come into the bathroom. I promise I won't muss you up."

"Oh, good grief," she muttered, her butterflies suddenly kicking up as he took her hand and they walked across the room.

"Put your elbows on the counter," he said firmly as he closed the door, "and scoot your feet back."

"I can't believe this."

"Sure you can," he said with a grin, carefully lifting her skirt and laying it over her waist. "Those are some pretty panties but I'm gonna pull them down to your thighs. There you go. Is that your hairbrush?"

"Why?"

"I'll take that as a yes," he quipped, shooting her a look. "I'm gonna give you a quick sting, and I can do that faster usin' that, but I'll be usin' my hand when we get back."

"Is that supposed to make me feel better?"

"Are you sayin' it doesn't?" he asked, picking up the oval wooden brush.

"I plead the fifth," she replied with a giggle.

"You want this just as much as I wanna give it to you. Go on, admit it."

"Never."

"You sure about that?" he asked, landing his first swat.

"Ouch. Okay, yes, I do, but damn that stings."

"Yep, like I said, this is faster, besides, you should know what it feels like."

He began peppering her bottom with quick, sharp taps, and though they were lightly applied, the speed of the delivery soon had its impact.

"Liam, ouch, ouch, ouch, please can you, ouch, stop now?"

"Sure, sugar. I'll pick this up again later," he declared pulling up her lacy underwear.

"Now I need a hug."

Opening his arms as she straightened up, she leaned against his chest. He could feel her melting into him, and suddenly, he didn't care about the party, or his famous guests, or anything else. All he cared about was how he felt at that moment.

Everything about it was perfect.

Though he was needed downstairs to greet his friends and clients as they arrived, he was lost in the amazing woman wrapped in his arms. He wanted to make love to her in her beautiful dress, and take an hour to peel it off her body.

"Don't we have to go soon?" she murmured, pulling back and gazing up at him. "Not that I want to. I want to stay right here, just like this, forever."

"Me too, except—now that I think about it—I could get myself arrested."

"Arrested? For what?"

"You look so damn gorgeous it'd be a crime to keep you outta the limelight."

"You always know the right thing to say, but I'm still nervous about meeting all those celebrities. You'll stick with me, right? "

"Are you kiddin'? I'm not gonna let you outta my sight. If I leave you for even a second, those singin' cowboys will be droolin' all over you as fast as a mule can kick."

"I doubt that, but thank you for saying it. Before we go I need to fix my lipstick and primp a bit."

"Just as well. If I stay here any longer we won't be leavin' at all, and I'm not kiddin'."

"Liam?"

"Yeah, sugar?"

"I love you."

"I love you too, baby."

Closing the door behind him, he started across the bedroom, but came to a sudden stop. A surge of heat had suddenly moved through his body.

"What the hell was that?" he muttered.

But even as the words left his lips, he sensed the evening had more surprises in store for him.

He just didn't know what they could be.

CHAPTER NINETEEN

The banquet doors opened at 9:00 p.m. All guests needed to be marked off the list and inside no later than 9:30 p.m. With so many people arriving in a short amount of time, a dozen hosts kept the flow moving. Those who were late would automatically be off the guest list the following year.

There were sound reasons behind Liam's strict policy.

Ensuring everyone's timely attendance prevented the awkwardness of early arrivals, it made it difficult for anyone not invited to sneak in, and Liam's authority was underscored. Being managed by his company virtually guaranteed success, but an artist had to play by Liam's rules. He had no compunction about terminating contracts if a client decided they knew better and began to throw tantrums.

Leaving the bedroom and entering the lounge, he spied Harry happily devouring an exotic sandwich. Liam liked him, but he suspected Harry was a canny, switched-on young man, not the naive youth he'd have people believe. As Liam drew closer, Harry took the last bite, then finished off a glass of beer.

"You only get two more through the evenin'," Liam said firmly, "so make them last."

Smiling, Harry placed the mug on the table in front of him.

"No wonder Summer likes you. She's had every guy she's ever dated wrapped around her finger, but I bet she can't steamroll her way over you."

Liam raised his eyebrows. His assessment of Harry was spot on.

"Getting back to the beer..." Liam replied, choosing to ignore the remark. "Two. That's it."

"Sure, no sweat."

"If anyone asks who you are, tell them your name, then say, I'm here as Liam's guest."

"Isn't everyone?" Harry said with a chuckle. "Sorry, I couldn't resist."

"Hey, I opened the door," Liam replied with a grin. "One more thing. You're a new face so people are gonna be curious. Just be yourself, and don't make stuff up. If they ask if you're a musician, tell them you're a classical pianist with a twist. It's the truth, and it's impressive, believe me."

"Thanks, Liam. I wasn't sure what to say. I mean, everyone here will be a country and western artist, right?"

"Mostly, but like I said, what you do is impressive. A couple of years from now they'll be talkin' about how they met you before you were famous."

"Seriously? You really think that's gonna happen?"

"Yep. I really do, Harry. Excuse me, here comes Summer."

* * *

As Liam moved swiftly across the room to greet his sister, Harry let out a heavy breath. Though he'd put up a brave front, even after a beer he remained unnerved. He'd never thought in a million years he'd be attending a New Year's Eve party in Nashville, let alone be sitting in the Presidential Suite of a luxury hotel and about to meet superstars.

And Liam Taylor believed in him.

The Liam Taylor.

Harry suddenly understood why the celebrated record producer and manager owned a jet and two homes at such a young age. Liam was clear about things. He was disciplined, focused and sharp, but more than anything, he was in control. Even with his difficult sister.

"I'm gonna be like you," Harry muttered to himself as Liam and Summer walked towards him. "I'm gonna be a musician, but I'm gonna be a smart musician. I'm gonna control things in my life. I'm not gonna let things control me."

"Hey, little brother," Summer said with a smile as she approached. "You look deep in thought."

"I am."

"I didn't know you were capable of it," she said with a laugh. "What's made you so serious?"

"Stuff."

"Okay, I get it, none of my business. Are you coming down with us?"

"Yeah," he nodded, removing the pendant around his neck and pushing it into his pocket. "I'm lookin' forward to this."

"You're gonna have a great time, Harry," Liam promised as they headed out, "and as for you, Summer Victoria Brown, I promise you an evenin' you'll never forget."

"It already is."

Two Hours Later

Summer was as bubbly as the champagne she'd been drinking. Meeting the stars she idolized and whose music she loved was thrilling. Harry had disappeared, but knowing Liam had someone watching over him she wasn't concerned.

Throughout the evening various artists had taken to the stage, and as her favorite band launched into one of their slow love songs, Liam swept her on to the dance floor. Moving to the slow, sensuous melody, his arms around her as he guided her around the floor, she was giddy with happiness.

"It's been a while since we were in the suite," he murmured as the song ended. "I should go up and socialize."

Leading her through the crowd and out of the banquet room, they ambled through the lobby to the elevators.

"Okay, but do you mind if I go back to the party?" she suddenly said as the doors opened. "I'm having too much fun."

"It getting late, Summer, and all you've had to eat are those tiny appetizer things. Trust me, you need more."

"I swear, I'm fine, I'm better than fine."

"Fine is a sunny day in May, and you are definitely buzzed. I don't wanna spoil your fun, sugar, but I need you sober."

"I am not ditzy," she protested as he bundled her inside and pushed the button. "Okay, maybe a teensy bit, but even if I am, I'm still fine."

"When we get to the suite you are gonna eat something substantial, even if I have to tie you to the bed and force-feed you."

"Ooh, I like that idea," she exclaimed, bursting into a fit of giggles. "Yes, let's do that."

"You think I'm kiddin'?"

"I hope not."

"Good grief. You're about as fine as a thunderstorm."

"What's with all the weather stuff? Hey, I know, let's go outside and walk naked in the rain. Wait—is it raining?"

"Oh, man, you're worse than I thought."

They reached their floor, and stepping out they started down the hallway, but halfway to the suite Liam abruptly stopped.

"Summer, when we go into that room you've gotta behave, you hear me? There are important people in there. You need to be a lady."

"I'm always a lady."

"Do I need to take you into the bathroom and whack your ass with that hairbrush to settle you down? I will if I have to."

"What? No, Sorry. I'll be normal."

"You're gonna sit down, and I'm gonna bring you something to eat. Tell me what I just said."

"I'm going to sit down, and you'll bring something to eat."

"And if a server offers you a glass of champagne, whatta you gonna do?"

"Say, no thank you."

"Correct. Let's go," he said, glancing at his watch. "We need to be downstairs by 11:45 p.m."

Though Liam's short, sharp lecture had helped, as they continued down the hall Summer's head still buzzed. The security guard at the door opened it for them, and moving inside she found the mellow music and quiet conversation a welcome change from the boisterous party in the banquet room.

As Liam walked her to one of several dining tables, she was surprised to see Harry across the room seated on a couch talking to a very pretty girl. The party was more his style.

"I'll be right back," Liam said, kissing her on the cheek and breaking into her thoughts. "I'll send a server over with some coffee."

"Thanks, Liam. Sorry. I think I have had a bit too much to drink."

"Yeah, you have, but that's okay. Some food and coffee will help."

As he headed off to the buffet table, she looked back at her brother. Harry turned and smiled across at her. She had never seen him so relaxed and confident. Even his posture was unfamiliar. Leaning back, he had his arm stretched along the top of the sofa, and one of his ankles rested on his knee. The attractive young woman leaned into him as she spoke, making it clear Harry was the one being pursued. He seemed to be taking it all in stride, as if beautiful girls crossed his path every day.

"Coffee for you, madame."

"Oh, thank you."

The waiter set down a full cup, along with a carafe, a small pitcher of cream, and a sugar bowl. Though she doctored the hot coffee and took a long drink, she couldn't take her eyes off her brother.

"Here," Liam said, placing a dish laden with chicken and vegetables covered in gravy in front her. "Eat it all."

"Thank you," she said gratefully, picking up her fork and diving into the mashed potatoes. "I didn't realize how hungry I was."

"Your brother appears to be havin' a good time."

"He certainly does. Who's the girl?"

"Irene McMillan," Liam replied, sitting down. "Her father is that gray-haired man over there. He's a State Senator."

"Oh, my gosh. Harry's hitting on a senator's daughter? I don't believe it."

"It looks to me like it's the other way around," Liam remarked with a grin. "Now stop talkin' and eat. We need to go downstairs in about fifteen minute, and I want you as clear-headed as possible."

"I had no idea how hungry I was, and you're right. I've been drinking on an empty stomach. I'm feeling better already."

But as Summer devoured her meal, Liam observed her brother and his confident demeanor. There was more to the young man than he allowed people to see, but Liam wasn't surprised. Harry was a classical pianist, and that required discipline and study.

"Wow, that was delicious," Summer declared, laying down her knife and fork. "Thank you."

"Are you okay to go back downstairs?"

"Absolutely. I feel almost normal."

"Good. I'll round up Harry and we'll go down together."

It was nearing 11:45 p.m.

The time for the big countdown approached.

* * *

Entering the banquet room, Summer couldn't believe her joke-cracking, smart-ass brother was conducting himself with such self assurance and panache. As Liam guided her through the throng, Harry followed suit, his arm protectively around the young woman at his side. The band came to the end of their song, and as they left to a rousing ovation, Liam continued forward, stopping directly in front of the stage.

"Harry, will you please stay with your sister for a minute."

"Sure."

"Summer," Liam said, solemnly, fixing her with a steady gaze, "stay right here. I've got a very big surprise for you."

"Really? Wonderful. I won't move from this spot."

But as he marched away, an unexcited chill pricked her skin.

"Harry, do you know anything about this?" she asked, grabbing her brother's arm.

"Nope, but don't worry, sis. If you need me, I'm here."

His arm came around her shoulder, and she knew he'd meant it, but he suddenly jerked his head up.

"Uh, Summer, Liam's on the stage."

As Liam strode up to the microphone, a hush fell over the crowd.

"Harry. What he's doing?"

"No idea, but we're about to find out."

"Evenin' everyone," Liam began. "Thanks for comin', and thanks to all of you who performed tonight. Weren't they great?"

The crowd roared and whistled, then quickly fell silent.

"As some of you know, I often use this night to introduce new talent. Usually they come up on the stage and perform. Trial by fire, you might say."

"You did that for me," a man's voice yelled from the crowd.

"Yep, I remember, Clint. You kicked ass and you've been kickin' it ever since, but this year's gonna be different. Get ready folks. This little lady is gonna take Nashville by storm, then the world."

A screen lowered on the stage.

The room fell dark.

Whispers and murmurs traveled through the crowd.

In the dim light, Summer could see Liam jump down from the stage and walk briskly towards her.

"Hey, sugar," he murmured, kissing her on the cheek.

"Who's going to—"

"Shush. You'll find out in a second."

A piano chord echoed through he room.

Harry caught his breath.

The screen came to life.

Leaning against the piano as Harry played behind her, an unseen saxophone floated into the melody, and Summer's image filled the screen.

"Liam," she whispered, "what...?"

But words failed her as the tears sprang from her eyes.

Life is a road we travel each day

Why am I always losing my way?
I miss the green light, I stop and I wait
Where do I turn? Is it all up to fate?
I have crashed a few times, no bruises to show
Other times I have sat and let tears freely flow
The aches leave, the cuts heal, but the scars remain
And each time I see you I remember the pain.
Cos you have the power to turn my tears into rain.
My tears into rain.
Love is lonely on a one-way street.
You're always ahead, how can we meet?
Love is hopeless on a one-way street
It burns in my chest with a white hot heat.
Life sends me forward, I can't turn back
I look over my shoulder, did I lose track?

Miles, like time, zip by me so fast
Will I leave you behind, lost in my past?
You look but don't see me
You listen but don't hear me
There's no love lost cos no love has been
found
I'm invisible because you won't turn around.
Living on hope, it can feel so empty
Will you become just another memory?
Should I exit now, before it's too late?
Or should I keep dreaming, should I still
wait?
Love is lonely on a one-way street.
You're always ahead, how can we meet?
Love is hopeless on a one-way street
And it burns in my chest with a white hot
heat.
Love is lonely on a one-way street.
Love is sad on a one-way street
Love is forsaken on a one-way street

Still it burns in my chest with a white hot
heat.
Each time I see you I remember the pain.
Cos you have the power to turn my tears in-
to rain.
My tears into rain.
My tears into rain.
Part the clouds, and let the sun dry the pain.

CHAPTER TWENTY

The last piano chord faded away. For a split second, silence hung over the room, then the crowd burst into loud applause. Moving her shocked eyes from the audience, Summer stared up at Harry, then threw her arms around Liam and buried her head in his chest.

"I think they'd like to meet you," Liam whispered as the lights came on and the screen rolled up.

"I c-can't stop sh-shaking," she stammered, fighting the overwhelming emotion. "I can't believe it, I just can't believe it."

"Get up on that stage and take the moment, sugar. You've got a whole lotta bows in your future, but this one is special. It's your first."

But summer was still trying to process what was happening. A crowd filled with famous singers were cheering for her and Harry.

"How is this possible? Am I dreaming?"

"Summer, you need to be on that stage," Harry insisted, placing his hands on her shoulders and turning her around. "Don't you realize you've just become a star? I'll go with you if you want, or go up with Liam, but go!"

"Would it be stupid if I said I need you both?"

"Not for a minute," Liam assured her, grabbing her hand. "Are you ready?"

"Fuck."

"I'll take that as a yes," Harry said with a grin, clutching her other hand.

With Liam and Harry on either side of her, they walked around the side of the stage and up the back steps. Gazing at the cheering throng, she took a deep breath, summoned her courage, and walked forward. As she stepped up to the microphone the applause reached a crescendo, and releasing her hands, Liam and Harry remained a few feet behind her.

"So, uh, I had no idea this was going to happen," she began hesitantly. "I'm totally terrified right now."

"Don't be, we love you," a voice yelled.

"Um, Thanks," she managed. "The piano player is my brother, Harry. He's an amazing musician, but I guess you all saw that."

"Harry, you rock," a male voice shouted.

"And you're hot too," a female added, causing a flurry of whistles.

"This is about as perfect as a dream could be," Summer continued, "except my folks aren't here. I suppose that sounds corny, but it's true."

"It's not corny. We get it. Keep talkin'," one of her all-time favorite singers shouted.

The woman was standing in front of the stage, and as Summer stared down at her, the singer raised her hand in a thumbs-up.

"Anyway, I come from a small town, and I had big dreams, but I never imagined I'd be on a stage at a big party like this, standing in front of all of you. Sorry," she mumbled, pausing to swallow back a sudden flood of emotion. "Obviously this is all because of Liam," she said, turning to look at him. "Liam, there isn't a thank you big enough for this incredible moment."

The crowd cheered again, shouting out his name.

"Um, about the song. The video you watched is from my youtube channel, It says the song is titled A One-Way Street, but it's actually called, A Song For Liam," she admitted nervously. "I had to set the record straight, so, uh, thank you everyone, for making this moment so amazing, and thank you, Harry, for being such a brilliant brother, and mom and dad, wherever you are, thank you for believing in me."

As she turned and walked away with Liam and Harry at her side, her song began playing, but not ready to head into the crowd she stood at the back of the stage in the shadows.

"I absolutely cannot believe this," she mumbled, clinging to Liam's arm as she stared across the room watching the guests sing along to the chorus.

"Hey, believe it. Your song is a hit, Harry's a hit, and you're a hit."

"How did you even know about my channel on YouTube?"

"Guilty," Harry piped up.

"What?"

"Someone had to tell him! Jeez, Summer, you'd been workin' at his house for months and hadn't said a word."

"How do you know that?"

"Well, duh! You would've talked my ear off."

"Harry," Liam said thoughtfully. "At the hospital—you didn't just let that slip? You purposely told me?"

"Guilty again," Harry said sheepishly. "Sorry about that. Kinda had to."

"And the sheet music on top of the piano?"

"I wanted you to look for that song when you found her on YouTube."

"Damn!" Liam muttered, shaking his head. "Harry, you're goin' a long way. You are something else!"

"Harry Brown! I want to hug you and choke you all at the same time," Summer declared. "You are so, so...conniving. Yes, that's the word. Conniving."

"The biggest stars in the business are singin' along with your song right now," Harry said, waving his arm at the audience. "Aren't you just a little bit glad?"

"A little bit glad?" she exclaimed, letting go of Liam and putting her arms around her brother. "Yeah, you could say that. Harry, you're the best."

As A Song For Liam ended, Auld Lang Syne seamlessly followed, waiters appeared carrying trays of champagne, and a ticking clock suddenly echoed through the room. Moments later, a deep male voice began speaking.

"Sixty-seconds folks. Grab the one you love, grab a glass, grab your streamers, grab whatever, and get ready for the countdown."

"Summer," Harry said hastily, "I'd really like to stay with you, but there's this girl I—"

"Go," Summer said quickly. "She's probably right where you left her hoping and praying you'll show up."

"Thanks. I'll see you upstairs in a few minutes."

As he raced away, Summer gazed up at Liam, losing herself in his milk-chocolate eyes.

"Ten! Nine! Eight!—"

"Happy New Year, Summer," Liam whispered in her ear as the countdown continued. "It's honestly the best I've had."

"Happy New Year, Liam. Me too."

Streamers and balloons fell from the ceiling, and locking his hands in her hair, he passionately devoured her mouth.

* * *

With the party winding down, Summer and Liam said their goodbyes, but she was still floating on a cloud. As they approached the door to the Presidential Suite they found the guard had left, and moving his arm from around her shoulders, Liam pulled out his card key.

"I'm still in shock, you know that, right?" she said happily. "I keep thinking this is just a dream and I'm going to wake up."

"It's no dream, sugar," he replied, pushing the door open and gesturing for her to go in ahead of him.

"It sure feels like—"

But she came to a sudden stop.

Her parents were hurrying forward to greet her.

"Mom? Dad?"

"Hello, sweetheart," her mother exclaimed, hugging her tightly. "You and Harry. My two babies, I was so proud I thought I was going to burst."

"Hey, kitten," her father said warmly, wrapping her up as Janet let her go. "That goes double for me."

"Where were you? When did you get here?" Summer asked breathlessly. "I thought you were going out to dinner somewhere. Didn't Liam arrange a car?"

"It was all part of the cover-up," Liam admitted. "Did you honestly think I'd let this night happen without your parents here?"

"I've been looking after them. Hi, I'm Marie, Liam's sister."

"I don't know what to say," Summer muttered, staring at the pretty brunette. "When I was standing on that stage I kept thinking, mom and dad should be here, and you were!"

"We spent the evenin' at Marie's home," Keith explained. "She brought us over just before the big moment, and what a moment it was!"

"I didn't think this could get any better, and it just did," Summer stammered, swallowing back more tears.

"We'll be stayin' the night here at the hotel, so we can get together for brunch tomorrow before we head back. I reckon you'll be too tired to get up in time for breakfast!"

"That is fantastic, except Harry should be here."

"I am," he said, tapping her on the shoulder. "I found them in the crowd right after I left you at the countdown."

"I'm going to start blubbering again," Summer declared. "It's too much. It's just too much."

"Please don't," Janet begged, hugging her again. "You'll get me started."

"There is one person that's missin'," Liam remarked, "and you've gotta tell me where I can find him."

"Who are you talking about?" Harry asked as the happy group moved into the room to sit down.

"The saxophone player."

"Uh, that would be me," Keith said quietly, appearing almost embarrassed.

Liam stared at him in shock, incredulous the muscled marine was the soulful sax player.

"I didn't wanna horn in on the kid's video, so I stayed off camera."

"That's funny dad," Harry said with a chuckle. "Horn in on the video! I'm stealin' that line."

"Keith, you're really good," Liam said earnestly. "You have to play on the CD."

"I still don't wanna steal their thunder."

"But you're part of their thunder."

"Please, dad, you have to," Summer pleaded, staring up at him with wide eyes. "It wouldn't be the same without you. Please…?"

"Oh, Lord, there it is. The look that melts me, but don't ask me to go on tour. I'm stayin' home with my best girl from now on," he said vehemently, taking Janet's hand.

"Forgive me, but I'm going to head off," Marie said, stifling a yawn. "Liam, will you walk me down?"

"Yeah, of course."

"Thanks again for everything, Marie," Keith said gratefully. "It was terrific."

"I had a blast. It was fun being part of a conspiracy."

As Liam and Marie left the room, Keith and Harry ambled to the buffet to sample the various cakes still set out, but sitting on the couch with Summer, her mother's gaze fell on the ruby ring.

"Heavens. That's gorgeous."

"Liam gave it to me. Isn't it beautiful?"

"It's more than beautiful. Summer…is there something you need to tell us?"

"Not yet. Well, sort of. It's a promise ring. Liam and I are officially an item."

"It matches your dress and your bracelet. How remarkable."

"Yeah, I know, but Mom, isn't he wonderful?"

"He sure is, sweetheart."

"I just hope I don't mess it up."

"Would you like some advice?"

"Mom, you can always give me advice."

"Never be afraid to tell him how much you love him, and make sure he always knows he's the only one for you."

"I knew it the moment he opened the door and I looked in his eyes. I know that sounds corny, but I got this feeling..."

"I know that feeling," her mother murmured with a soft smile, "and that magic, whatever it is, will help you through the rough spots, but you must learn how to forgive and forget. Forgetting isn't easy sometimes, but that's the key."

* * *

A little while later, lying in bed curled into each other's arms, though exhausted from the thrilling evening Liam and Summer were too wired to sleep.

"Liam, what happens now?" Summer asked softly. "I mean with my song and everything? How does it all work?"

"My legal department will draw up a contract. You need your own lawyer to review it, and once it's signed we go into the studio, though your contract might raise some eyebrows."

"Why?"

"Cos there's gonna be a hairbrush clause!"

"Liam!" she exclaimed, giggling as she punched his arm.

Abruptly pulling the covers back, he sat up, grabbed her wrist, and deftly yanked her over his lap.

"Liam! What the hell?" she squealed, staring at him over her shoulder.

"It may not be in writin', but I'm puttin' you on notice right now!" he declared, landing a solid smack.

"Ow!"

"If you get too big for your britches," he continued, moving his slaps from cheek to cheek, "I'll spank your butt 'til it's as red as your ruby ring."

"Ouch, ow, okay, I get it."

"I mean it, Summer," he said sternly, continuing to rain his flattened palm across her backside. "When I put on my management hat I'm the boss."

"Ow, ow, I'll be a good girl!"

"It's your beautiful bottom that will pay the price if you don't. Do we understand each other?"

"Yes, but I can't be perfect all the time," she bleated as he rubbed her scorched skin. "That would be boring."

"You could never be borin'," he muttered, slipping his hand into her pussy and rubbing her clit. "Difficult and a smart-ass, but never borin'."

"Liam..." she breathed, wriggling against his touch, "please make love to me."

"I haven't heard sir in a while," he remarked, pinching her cheeks.

"Yes, Sir," she said hastily. "Sorry. I forgot."

"Next time you're over my knee and it slips your mind I'll remind you," he declared, landing a hot swat, "but I'll do it with more than the palm of my hand."

"Ow! Yes, Sir."

"What is it you want?"

"Please, Sir, will you make love to me?"

With his stiffened cock craving her, he swiftly moved her off his lap, rolled her on her back, and clutched her breasts. Diving his mouth to her nipples and ravenously drawing them in, Jason Aldean's hit song suddenly blasted through his mind.

I've never met a girl like you...

"What's wrong?" she asked as he abruptly lifted his head.

"Nothin'. I just need to grab a condom."

"No, please don't."

He paused.

"Aren't you worried?"

"That you have some horrible disease? Are you kidding? You're way too careful, and I know I'm okay."

"But darlin', what—"

"If I got pregnant? I'd be the happiest girl in the world—but I guess that's scary for you."

"Takes a lot to scare me, sugar," he quipped with a grin, "but we're gonna have a lot on our plate this year. Don't worry. I know what to do."

Straddling her body, he stared into her sapphire blue eyes, took hold of his naked member, and placed it at her entrance. It had been years since he'd been inside a woman without the thin shield, and as he thrust forward, the delicious feel of his cock inside her hot, wet pussy sent the blood rushing through his loins.

"Liam, you feel incredible."

"Damn, baby..."

It was all he could manage.

Unable to stop himself, he quickened his pace, then abruptly lowered his lips on hers in a fervent kiss. Her muffled moans rang in his ears as his member pummeled her pussy, and though he didn't want the moment to end his climax was already threatening. He had to push the pause button.

"No, please," she begged as he withdrew and broke their kiss. "Please, Sir, don't stop."

"I'm not ready for this to end," he growled, slowly pushing back in.

Watching her squeeze her eyes shut and bite her lower lip, he continued his measured thrusts, then suddenly pulling out, he grabbed her ankles and flipped her over. Taking hold of her hips, he plunged back inside, but continuing the leisurely strokes, he reached beneath her and massaged her clit.

She let out a plaintive wail, urging him on.

He rubbed harder and pumped with more force.

She threw back her head and arched her back.

"Ask!" he ordered, moving his hand from her sex and spanking her with quick, hot slaps.

"Please, Sir, may I come? Please, oh, please."

Her shrill request sent a rush of energy through his cock.

Tightening his grip, he thrust with abandon.

"Come now!"

With a euphoric cry, she bucked beneath him, pushing him over the edge. Grabbing his cock and snatching it from her depths, he spewed his essence across her crimson behind with loud, guttural groans, then breathlessly collapsed beside her.

EPILOGUE

Harry met with Scott Bridges at Scott's home studio before returning to Apple Valley. The hour Scott had put aside became the entire afternoon. They jammed, discussed their favorite artists, and when the time came for Harry to leave, neither wanted the meeting to end.

That night, on his return flight home, Harry made up his mind to drop out of college.

Spending three years studying subjects the college forced him to take to graduate with an arts degree seemed like a waste of time. It was three precious years he could be making music with a truly great producer. Fully prepared to do battle when he faced his parents, he was shocked when his father accepted his decision.

"I thought you'd give me hell," Harry exclaimed. "I don't understand."

"Scott called! We talked!" Keith said solemnly. "He said he's been lookin' for a talent like yours for years. Long story short, he's ready to go full steam ahead, and he claims he knows the right people to get your special brand of music into the mainstream. Harry, he thinks you're gonna blow people's minds. I couldn't be prouder, son."

As his father and mother both hugged him, for the first time in his young life Harry experienced a well of emotion that made it difficult to speak.

"So, uh, how will this work?" he managed as they broke away. "Scott's in Nashville and I'm here."

"He wants you to move out there and stay in his guest house," Janet sniffled, quickly adding, "It's simply wonderful, but I'll miss you. My two babies are all grown up, and it just seems like yesterday you were both running around this house getting into all sorts of mischief."

"Mom..."

"Don't worry, Harry. I couldn't be happier for you. These are proud, joyful tears."

"Anyway," Keith interjected, wanting to relieve the emotional moment, "your mother and I have talked about it, and we'll use your college fund to see you through until you start earnin'. From the sounds of it, that won't take long," Keith continued, placing his arm around his wife, "Scott will be bookin' you some gigs pretty quick. When you're ready, and Liam's house is finished, Scott wants to use that studio to record. I have a feelin' we'll be seein' you back here sooner than you might think."

"Now I know how Summer feels," Harry muttered, staring at his parents in disbelief. "I feel like I'm livin' a dream."

* * *

Summer and Liam's relationship blossomed, but there were times she was needed in Apple Valley. With the severe winter weather abating, the renovations was making fast progress, and Summer had to view the construction firsthand. She was always thrilled to be home and with her parents, but with each visit she became increasingly aware she belonged in Nashville with Liam.

The choice for her first single had been obvious. *A Song For Liam,* but selecting the songs for her debut album hadn't been quite so easy, and there had been more than a few quarrels. Lying in bed late one night after a particularly stormy disagreement, Liam flashed back to the conversation they'd had just a few short months before on New Years Eve.

If you get too big for your britches I'll spank your butt 'til it's as red as your ruby ring. I mean it, Summer. When I put on my management hat I'm the boss."

He abruptly realized he hadn't lived up to his promise!

Rolling on top of her, he took hold of her wrists and held them at the sides of her head.

"Listen real careful. I know what I'm doin'. You're gonna have to trust me."

"But—"

"Don't interrupt!" he said sharply. "I'm not gonna spend any more time arguin' with you. You blew everyone away with your performance on New Year's, and you're gigs are bringin' in new fans, but time is marchin' on. I'm not gonna sit around quibblin' about song choices when I know what's right. Dammit, Summer, we've gotta jump on this momentum."

"Liam, I know the lyrics that touch me, and the ones that—"

"You can stop right there. We both know you can sing the socks off any song when you put your mind to it."

"Well, yeah," she murmured softly, widening her eyes, "but—"

"Lookin' at me with those big baby blues of yours and tryin' to get your way isn't gonna work!" Suddenly sitting up, he jerked her over his lap and slapped her backside. "Tomorrow I'll make the final cut. Got it?"

"Ouch. Yes, Sir!" she said hastily. "Whatever you think, though Heart Stopping Love is—"

"Dammit!" he exclaimed, spanking her with gusto.

"Okay, okay, please stop! I won't argue anymore, I swear."

"You always have to push the dang envelope," he grunted. "I'm puttin' you on maintenance. Recordin' is fun and excitin', but it can be a whole lot tougher than pickin' out a few songs. Startin' right now, I'm spankin' you once a week."

"Ow, oh, Sir. You don't have to!"

"Hush up. Maintenance is gonna save us both a lotta trouble. Any more objections?

"Ouch. No, Sir."

"Then stay still and be grateful," he declared, quickening the force and pace of his slaps. "I'll be hirin' top notch musicians, and they don't take kindly to divas."

"Ow, oh, Sir, I'll be good, I promise."

"Heatin' up your butt once a week will see to that."

Whisking his hand across her sit spot, he delivered a flurry of stinging swats eliciting several loud yelps.

"That's it, you're done," he declared, smoothing his hand over her red seat with a comforting caress, "but you'll be back over my lap one week from now. If you give me any trouble in the next seven days, I'll add a hairbrush or maybe my belt. Are we clear?"

"Yes, Sir," she replied breathlessly. "I won't."

"I should've tanned your hide after that first tantrum," he muttered, "but never fear, sugar, I won't let that happen again."

Continuing to rub away the sting, he waited until she let out a long sigh and sank into his lap, then helped her stretch out next to him and brought her into his arms.

"You got anything to say?"

"Thank you," she murmured, melting against him, "and I'm sorry I've been so difficult."

"You're welcome, sugar," he said softly, holding her tightly.

"It's so weird how that works."

"Gettin' your butt spanked?"

"I hate to admit it," she whispered, "but it does calm me down. You really are my hero."

"Are you ready to hear some good news? I haven't had a chance to tell you."

"Yes, for sure," she murmured, moving her head to look up at him. "What's happened?"

"I heard from Ted. The guest house will be finished in about two weeks."

"That's fantastic. I'm not surprised. The last time I was there, except for all the plastic sheeting, it looked almost livable. Does this mean we can record there? You still want to, right?"

"You bet. I can't wait to get back in my studio. I'd better start nailin' down the musicians, but, Summer, like we talked about, I'm not messin' with the single. Just your dad on the sax and Harry on the piano. Damn, I just got chills. I predict a Platinum record."

"Honestly?"

"Yep, I don't say things I don't mean."

He stared at her for a moment, then lowered his lips on hers in a long, lingering kiss.

"Mmm, what was that for?" she asked softly.

"Summer," he began, his voice low, "I wanna make that ring official. I love you, and—"

"Oh, my gosh, yes, the biggest yes ever!"

"Damn, girl, I didn't get to finish."

"Sorry. Go ahead. Pretend I kept my mouth shut...please...?" she begged, widening her eyes and gazing up at him.

"You and your baby blues," he muttered, shaking his head.

"Please will you keep going? I won't make a peep."

"You'd better not," he said, fixing her with a warning glare, then taking a deep breath, he ran his fingertip around her face. "Damn, you're beautiful. Summer,I love you, and I wanna spend the rest of my life lovin' you. Will you marry me sugar, and spend the rest of your life lovin' me?"

She paused, then taking a deep breath, she began to sing.

"I wished and I dreamed,
I lied and I schemed.
But you forgave my past.
Now you're mine at last.
When you hold me,
And your lips brush mine
It's meant to be.
It's love sublime
Heaven on earth, it really is true
A miracle happened. That miracle's you."

"Damn, girl," he managed, fighting a rush of heat in his throat, "you just took my breath away."

"I started writing it on the plane during my last trip, but we've been so busy I haven't been able to finish it. I want to now, very badly. I'd love to include it if you think it's good enough."

"It already is, except, I'm not the miracle, sugar, we are...in fact..." he murmured thoughtfully, "I've been tryin' to think of a name for the album. That's it! Miracles!"

"The way you found me in my car—escaping the avalanche—that deputy finding us—"

"And the ring," he interjected. "Not just how it fit your finger, but how it matched your dress and bracelet."

"Miracles," she whispered. "You're right. It's perfect."

"Perfect," he repeated, "and with all our flaws, that's what we are together, sugar. Miraculously perfect."

THE END

A WORD FROM MAGGIE

If you liked this book (or even if you didn't), I would really appreciate you leaving a review on the site from which it was purchased. Reviews provide useful feedback, and allows me to work even harder to provide you with the very best reading experience I can offer.

Visit Me

http://www.MaggieCarpenter.com

www.facebook.com/MaggieCarpenterWriter

www.twitter.com/magcarpenter2[1]

Write to Maggie at:

MagCarpenter@yahoo.com

---

1. http://www.twitter.com/magcarpenter2

BOOKS BY MAGGIE CARPENTER

#1 AMAZON BESTSELLER
ROUGH COWBOY
HUNKS and HORSES
(Featuring characters from COWBOY: His Ranch. His Rules. His Secrets)
A FOUR BOOK SERIES - HEA - STANDALONE
TO KISS A COWBOY
TO CATCH A COWBOY
TO CON A COWBOY
TO TRUST A COWBOY
SEXY SCIFI - PARANORMAL
ROUGH ALPHA
TRAINED BY THE ALIEN
WARLOCK
THE ALIEN'S RULES
BDSM CONTEMPORARY ROMANCE
ROUGH ROAD
ROUGH ROCKSTAR
THE STRICT BRITISH BARRISTER: BOOKS 1 & 2
SINS BEHIND THE SCENES
I AM A DOMINANT
DESIRE UNLEASHED - Sexsomnia
TIMELESS OBSESSION
For a full list of her novels visit her author page.
https://www.amazon.com/author/maggiecarpenter

www.ingramcontent.com/pod-product-compliance
Lightning Source LLC
Chambersburg PA
CBHW050736230626
47052CB00002BA/367